When The Rain Falls

Book 1 of Wicked Wayz

By Aries Ghost

Chapter 1

It was early Saturday morning . The sun was beginning to shine through the branches of the giant oak in the corner of the cemetery at St. Malachi's . Rays of light and shadow danced over the gatherers at Samantha Rain's last social event , her funeral . The crowd was sparse but varied , Brad Creed and Lily Hill flirting when they thought no one was looking , Sam's fellow librarian Danny Arco and his younger sister Veronica , a man dressed in rags helping himself to the food , and a few others to round it out .

Samantha Rain Tanor was the wife of Sheriff Mathew Tanor , mother and best friend to their girls Casidy and Zia . She was the quintessential church going wife , super mom , community volunteer . She was well respected by her peers , that is until she was caught pleasuring her self with a lit black candle while lying in the midst of Bakers Forrest . She had glyphs painted on her stomach and the insides of her spread legs . The entire congregation of St. Malachi's knew with in a couple of days . Gossip of witchcraft and wickedness spread and Sam became shunned by most of her former peers . Three days later she took her own life , jumping to her death from Spencer bridge .

Her closed casket sat before a six foot hole . It was cheap and simple , barely more than a pine box . Her tombstone a small marker on the ground with the words "Sam lies here" . No viewing , no pomp and circumstance , just the closure to a tragic life .

"Damn this sun , aren't funerals supposed to happen on cold gloomy days ? " Thought deputy Grace Smitter as she wiped the sweat from her face while walking to her car for a smoke . Her hips had a forceful sway as she moved , her short brown hair bouncing in synch . As she reached the parking lot , Mathew approached her .

"Thank you for coming Grace , I am starting to feel closed in with all these people and their false pleasantries . "

"Of course I came , I would never abandon you in your

time of need sir . I am here for you . " A gentle smile crossed her face as she leaned in and embraced him . " I would do any thing for you Mathew . I hope you know how much you mean to me . "

" Of course I do . "

" You have my house key . Why don't you chill at my place and get some rest when this is over . I will come check on you when I finish my patrol . " Grace smiled and kissed him on the cheek .

" Sounds like a good idea . I can't deal with the girls today . "

She released her embrace and continued her journey for her nicotine fix , glancing back briefly to smile at him .

Daniel and Veronica stood restlessly by their seats . He was in his mid thirties , medium height and build . Ash hair cut plain . Square rimmed glasses covering his green eyes . She was a mere five two , ten years her brothers junior . Black hair pulled into a pony tail that reached her waste . Both were dressed in black out of respect .

" I am so sorry about Sam . I know how much you loved her . "

" Don't worry about me . I am fine . "

" I hope those girls will be ok . "

Daniel looked up into the sky . " They will be . Sam raised them . "

A young lady in her early twenties approached them . She had shock white hair and vibrant blue eyes . She was taller than Veronica at five six and walked in a calm but sure manner . She donned a black skirt and jacket , a white silk shirt beneath it .

" Oh , hello Persephone . How are the girls ? " Veronica asked .

" I am only their baby sitter , then again with their fathers mood of late , I am probably all they have . " She looked at the ground and sighed . " But they will get through this . That I know . "

" Sorry . I saw the girls ride in with you and figured , you know . "

" Ya . It's cool . I do adore them and I would do anything for them . " She smiled and rolled her eyes .

" Oh by the way , I Put Sam's effects from work in the back seat of your car . Sorry for being presumptuous . " Daniel grinned and patted Persephone on the shoulder . " I know they will fine as long as they have you . "

Persephone's eyes began to water . She took a deep breath and turned around . She glanced back at them . " Thanks . I am sure the girls will appreciate their mom's stuff . I will catch you later . " She slowly walked away to find her seat .

Mathew walked back to the gathering , scanning the scene to locate his girls , when a cold hand touched his shoulder from behind .

"There you are sheriff , I came to tell you Victor will be here shortly to say some words for Sam , he felt it right , even considering the horrible circumstances surrounding her death . "

Mrs. Margaret Solomon , wife of Reverend Victor Solomon of St. Malachi's , was a short plump woman . She had a voice that would rattle the dead . Her nose was for ever pointed to the heavens and her eyes down at her lessors , which was most every one according to her .

"I just can't understand why she did what she did , she had a loving family and a community that adored her , yet she just threw it all away along with her immortal soul "

"Believe me Margaret , I am as baffled as you are , I thought I knew my wife . I just want to get this day over with and put it all behind me . I need to find my girls . "

"Of course , let Victor or I know if there is any thing we can do for you or the girls . "

Mathew forced a smile as he quickly departed the scene and made his way toward toward the other gatherers in search of his girls .

Zia was standing before her mothers casket muttering something incoherent . A single tear ran down her face as she brushed her coal black hair from her face to reveal her deep blue eyes and the perpetual look of curiosity in them . "What is death ? " she thought to her self , the realization of

*lessor means landlord, did you mean lesser ?(inferior)

one thing came to her , that she could never discuss such things with her mother any more for she had left this world . Another tear fell at that thought . She brushed it away as she turned and made her way to her seat . Zia knew things would change now and that she had to grow up quick , she pondered this as she sat down , trying to hold back yet another tear that demanded it's release .

"It's alright to cry sweetheart " Persephone said as she brushed the side of Zia's face , "Letting your tears fall will make you feel better , keeping them caged causes them to stir making matters linger inside causing you even more grief "

"I know Persephone , but they seem to be in single file line , escaping one at a time , it will take them awhile to all evacuate my eyes " A slight smile crossed her face at the thought of her clever words .

"Your too much little girl , it's a pleasure being your babysitter and friend "

"Thanks , I'm glad you came with us , mom would be happy to know you care " and with that she embraced Persephone and the tears began to flow more liberally .

"I will be with you as long as you need me sweet thing , as long as you need me "

Under the giant oak sat another girl . Silent and unmoving she peered at the crowd . Her face contorted with both grief and anger . Her short blond hair failing to cover her pain . Her deep blue eyes fell accusingly on the whispering flock of people as they made their social dance amongst each other , speaking to one another with vacant smiles as they pretended to hold back tears . She had already cried out all the tears she could produce and now felt only emptiness and numbness and a sick feeling in the pit of her stomach .

" I failed you mom , I am so sorry " , She wiped her eyes .
" I'll never forgive them for the way they made you feel , I'll never forgive him . Who will I talk to now about things I don't understand ? Who will make me feel better now that you are gone ? Selfish Casidy , it's not about you . I am so sorry . Please forgive me mom . I miss you "

" Where is your sister , Zia " Mathew asked as he took his seat .

She pointed to the oak tree as she softly spoke " Dad , you might want to leave her be , she has been there since we arrived and has not spoken to any one "

" Fine , I have enough to deal with . "

"She needs time is all . " Interjected Persephone .

"I suppose you are right , it is hard enough dealing with my own grief than to add hers to the mix "

"Typical " , thought Zia wondering if she had said it out loud .

The crowd began to settle into their seats as Reverend Solomon made his way to the podium . He opened his bible and began to read verse after verse pulled from various books , he strung them together into a poetic rant that depicted god's great love and the promises of salvation . As he continued on , the tone of his words got darker , warning of temptations and unforgivable sins . In the midst of his words , he was drawn to silence from an out burst from behind .

"Liars and hypocrites , that's what all of you are ! " The voice echoed from beneath the giant oak . "You talk about love and forgiveness , yet all of you drove her to her end , I blame all of you , murderers! "

With a glare aimed at the shocked on lookers , Casidy stormed toward the gates of the cemetery , her dry eyes once again pouring wetness , resolved not to look behind her to see the confusion she left in her wake , she picked up her pace .

As Casidy exited the cemetery , Zia and Persephone got to their feet .

" We will get her sheriff and I'll take the girls home just stay and get Sam buried , alright ? "

" Thank you Persephone . I will not be home tonight . Will you watch them until tomorrow ? I need time to get my head straight . "

" Of course , any thing to help the girls "

Persephone and Zia headed out the gate to find Casidy

who was sitting in Persephone's car already , shaking and crying . They climbed in and made their way out of St . Malachi's .

" I am so sorry for that " Mathew said in an irritated voice as he looked around at every one .

"It is alright " spouted Victor , " Grief causes some of us to act irrationally , give her time she will come around " and with that he smiled and began making his way toward the church . " I will be near if you need to talk Mathew , come see me when ever when ever you want to . "

The rest of the gatherers took the hint and began to rise and made their way to their cars . Mathew could here the whispers crossing their lips as they made light of the events that preceded , with an occasional chuckle of ridicule over a funeral that should not have been and the crazy girl that made it entertaining .

The caretaker took it as a sign as well and began lowering the casket into the ground with a shovel at his side for the long nights work .

Chapter 2

Kaid's orphanage , home of Eric Kaid and his nine charges .
It was an older building sitting near the end of Talon road .
The paint had been worn off by years of weather and no
one caring enough to keep it fresh . The front door hung
slightly tilted on a sagging frame . Half the windows were
boarded up while the other half had panes of cracked glass .
The yard looked post apocalyptic , with sparse vegetation
dotting bare dirt and rock contrasting the lush forest not
fifty yards away . The train tracks ran on the other side of
the road . If there was a wrong side of the tracks , this was
it . But this was the kids home and they cherished it . The
roof above kept them dry and the floors supported their
bed rolls for sleep time .

Eric came to the county and started the orphanage nine
years ago . He brought two of his charges with him ,
Domino at four years of age and Vander at seven . The
others came to him over the next three years ending with
Alexis brought to him as an infant . He has devoted his
entire life since then solely to their care .

It was another lazy Saturday morning , a day to play and
renew them selves after a hard week of summer lessons
given by Eric . He was strict when it came to learning , but
enjoyed pampering the kids when he could afford it . " My
kids will have bright futures " , he would tell people , "
Learning is the key and they do like to learn "

He awoke at 8 am sharp , letting himself sleep an extra
hour on the week ends .The smell of bacon and toast
caressed his nose as his eyes opened , " Stacy is cooking
breakfast , yep it's Saturday " he thought to himself as he
slowly rose to his feet . He put his casuals on and headed
down stairs to fill his stomach before the rest of the kids
awoke and and devoured everything .

" Good morning Stacey , smells divine as usual . " He told
the girl as he grabbed a plate .

She was small for sixteen with amber hair mostly covering

her green eyes and a voice that radiated with kindness .

"He-he , you say the same thing every Saturday morning Mr. Kaid " , she said as she laid two eggs sunny side up upon his plate " and you are always the first one to sample my cooking "

" I'm not here to sample young lady , I'm here to fill my tummy with yummy food crafted by our resident master chef "

As he put the first bite in his mouth a smile broke across his face and the look of satisfaction gleamed in his eyes .
" You really know how to start my week end the right way , I do so enjoy a good breakfast "

Stacey blushed as she turned back to the stove to begin cooking for the rest of her mates . " I enjoy cooking for every one , it makes me feel needed and I enjoy being needed , maybe some day I'll be a good mom . "

He could only respond with a smile since his mouth stayed crammed with food and politeness kept him from speaking to her . He nodded and turned his focus back to his now half full plate .

"Right on , chow time " came a soft little voice from the foot of the stairs .

" Morning Alexis my little angel " , Stacey's smile grew brighter at the first sign of life from the stairs , as she began preparing a plate for her young friend . " One Alexis special coming up " . She had learned all her mates favorite foods and tried to provide a special breakfast for each of them on Saturdays based on what was in the fridge and cupboards .
" For you half a grapefruit with sugar on top , an egg hard fried and a glass of powdered milk "

"Sounds sweet , bring it on I'm starved " the 6 year old sat next to Eric , eagerly awaiting her morning fuel . Holding her fork in one hand and Ms. Pink , her teddy in the other , she was ready to start her day . As Stacey put the plate down Alexis showed her talents . She scarfed down her meal one handed , never letting go of Ms. Pink , and finished before Eric could swallow and say good morning .

" Yay , I'm full now and ready to go , going out side to play now " and with that she darted out the door to the sun filled world out side , Ms. Pink apparently going with the flow dangling from her left hand ready to fade into a slightly whiter pink beneath the rays of light from the heavens .

As one darted outside another appeared at the base of the stairs . Eyes half open young Ivan let out a yawn .

" Morning young man , I have a book for you from the library , it is sitting on the table by the door "

Ivan's eye came wide open as he made his way to the table where a book on astronomy was sitting waiting for his inspection .

" Thanks Mr. Kaid " he said as he grabbed the book and made his way to his breakfast waiting in Stacey's hand .

" There you go little bit "

She patted him on the head as she handed him scrambled eggs on toast .

He took his food and book and headed to his usual corner in the back of the house .

" I've never met an eight year old that liked reading as much as he does , nor an adult for that matter . Speaking of reading , the others should be rising in a few " Eric said as he stood up and wiped his mouth , " I'll be on the bench out front reading the new adventure novel I got from the library "

"Very well Mr. Kaid , I'll make sure every one gets their breakfast , enjoy your book , its a wonderful day out ."

Eric made his way out the door and to the only tree the yard had , beneath it was his bench . Many of book has been read from this perch , sometimes for his own leisure but mostly to the children on nice days like today . He observed Alexis sitting on the ground , Ms. Pink before her . She was using rocks as tea cups and plates , referring to her teddy as your highness as she served her pretend tea in pretend tea cups .

" She has a vivid imagination " he thought as he pealed open the first page of his book and with in moments he could hear the sounds of footsteps flying down the stairs . "

Yep . Made it out here just in time . It is going to be an interesting day . " He looked down at the page before him and began to read . A smile crossed his face as he flipped the page .

Chapter 3

As the car pulled into the driveway Zia cheered " Finally , we are home . That was a long ride . "

" The farther away that place is from me the better . " Casidy replied harshly .

" I didn't mean anything by it sis . "

" I know . I am sorry Z . I just don't feel right at the moment , I just want to go to my room and crash . "

The girls exited the car . Zia grabbed Casidy's hand as they made their way to the front door .

" I'll let you slide with being grumpy for a bit ok ? "

" Thanks . Don't ever change . "

She tried to smile for Zia but only managed to loosen her frown some .

Persephone unlocked the door and the girls filed in behind her . Casidy made her way to her room and closed her self away from the world out side it . Zia stared at Casidy's door and shook her head "

" I hope she feels better . I hate seeing her like this . "

" She will be fine . She has you looking after her . Now go get changed while I pour me a drink sweety . " She swatted Zia on the ass . " Go on . I really need that drink . I will fix us a fantastic lunch in a few minutes . "

Her charge understand and headed to her room to get changed and wash up while giving her friend time to unwind .

Persephone made her way into the den where she scanned Mathew's bar for a suitable mood enhancer , two shades of rum , a Russian vodka , whiskey from the local brewery and a bottle of tequila barely touched , the worm at the bottom looking lonely and very still .

" I think the Russians know their poisons " she said to her self as she grabbed the bottle and poured a tumbler half full . She made her way to the kitchen to finish it off with ice and an orange slice . Upon returning to the den , she fell onto the cushy couch and took her first gulp . " one" she blurted . Two through five went by quickly followed by the word empty and a brisk smile crossed her face . She looked around the room examining it as if she had never been here before . The maple bar which had become her friend when the mood struck her , an antique desk and chair with papers lying about on top , the knock off oriental rug covering the den floor .

" I hate this room , it is where dad spends most of his off time "

She glanced over her shoulder , holding an empty glass , to see Zia standing at the door wearing black silk shorts and top with a splatter of blue butterflies .

" I wonder what he would say if he knew you invaded his bar ?"

" Well sweet thing , the room isn't going to tell him are you ? "

Zia smiled , " We both know the answer to that . How about that food you promised ? "

Persephone got up from her retreat , washed her glass and returned it to its proper spot then moved to Zia to embrace her . " I am a little tipsy so I'm ready to serve . " She let go and headed to the kitchen with a small sway to her step . " Sit down and relax " she yelled as she vanished through the kitchen door .

Zia made her self comfortable in the living room in her mom's recliner . She began riffling through the magazines under the end table next to the chair . " House wife stuff , not interested " she mumbled as she realized the futility of finding any worthy reading material . Her thoughts were suddenly rattled by the sound of glass breaking in her father's den . She quickly got up and headed to investigate .

" Felix ! , bad cat ! " , she yelled after seeing shattered tumblers on the floor and her cat dancing across the bar . " Are you trying to get me in trouble you silly thing ? " She grabbed him by the scruff of his neck and escorted him to the door , lightly tossing him to the brutal world out side . " You will sleep out here tonight for misbehaving . "

Felix began his serenade of pleas and apologies but only

met with his mistress shutting the door and leaving him to fend with the elements . He was a gorgeous blue fur cat , a black bandana with butterflies wrapped around his neck . He had been with her for over seven years now , a gift from Sam on her sixth birthday and he knew when he had messed up . She only put him outside when he pissed her off and that was not often . He gave up his song of woe knowing she was ignoring him and decided to make a day of it . He headed down to the creek and began to run west down its banks in search of something to entertain him .

" What was all that noise ? It sounded bad . " Persephone inquired as she sat two plates of spaghetti on the table .

" Spaghetti , that's your fantastic meal ? "

" It is when you are tipsy . The noise ? "

" That was my supposed friend trying to cause me more woe today . Felix broke some of dads tumblers so I threw his butt out the door . "

" Harsh . Did he break the one I was using ? "

" I think so since only one was left untouched , why ? "

" I will have to thank him then for destroying my finger prints before your dad dusted them . '

" Wow , you are funny when you drink . "

" Just when I drink ? , I'll have to raid your dad's bar more often . "

Zia began to laugh and sat to feast on her *fantastic* meal . " Thanks for always trying to make me feel better , you are the best baby sitter a girl could ask for . "

" I've been meaning to ask , what is it with you and butterflies ? " Persephone sat down and stared intently at Zia waiting for her answer .

" They are the perfect metaphor for life . They come into this world in the midst of chaos and struggle toward adulthood , unknowing what lies in their future . Then one day they wrap them selves up in a cocoon and emerge an adult ready for the pleasures and sorrows it is due . "

" Are you sure you are only thirteen , that is pretty deep . So which are you caterpillar or butterfly ? "

" I am in a cocoon I think . I do not care about childish

things any more but I am still trying to figure out what makes you grown ups do the things you do . Mom liked butterflies also . " Zia replied as she began inhaling the food before her .

" Ah , now that is a good reason to like something " . Persephone gave her young friend a sly smile as she turned her attention to her plate .

Chapter 4

" You have been reading that book for awhile Eric . It must be good "

Violet had her hands locked behind her back . Leaning over his shoulder licking her lips . She was wearing hand me down clothing as where the rest of the kids , yet on her they looked like high fashion . Her long black hair pulled into a tight pony tail , her soft eyes the color of her name sake .

" You get a little older , I worry for the boys whose hearts you will break "

" How much older is a little older " she inquired , " I'll be 15 soon , is that old enough to break hearts " a wicked smile crossed her face as Eric began to blush .

" Young lady stop teasing , I'm to old to handle your clever ways " He said with a faint laugh , " You have a few years yet before you should start thinking of such things "

" Ouch , well you brought it up now didn't you " , her smile turned into a tight frown , " I'll go sit in front of the mirror and practice being an old maid then "

She turned her back to him and sashayed back into the house causing Eric to wonder why he opened his mouth to start with . He shivered at the thought of dealing with that girl in a couple of years then returned to unfolding the story that was before him .

The parlor was cool . A breeze was blowing through the open front door . The light flickered above the two young people looking down at the pile of chips before them .

" Geez Domino , can't you let me win just one game . " Nick cried as he threw his cards down on the floor . " Your just frikin impossible to beat . "

" No , it is just impossible for you to beat me silly . " his nemesis snapped backed .

" Very funny . One more game , but this time you play with your eyes closed . "

Domino's gray eyes fell sharply on Nick as she

contemplated whether he was serious or not . She had on a simple white dress trimmed in blue plaid . Her blond hair flowed to her waist . She got up from up from the floor and began brushing the dust of her ass .

" May be later . " She told him as she made her way to the kitchen for something to nibble on .

Reginald was there leaning with his back to the counter top . He was a tall and slender with more facial hair than most sixteen year old boys . His ash hair in short dreadlocks .

" Yo Domino , whats cooking sugar ? "

She began softly growling at him . " I told you to quit talking to me like that . Can you not form a proper sentence slacker ? Seriously . "

" Woe is me . You really know how to shatter a guys ego . Man you are viscous for thirteen mistress Domino . " As he spoke he stepped out of her reach anticipating a violent reaction .

" Sigh . You are impossible . I am just going to ignore you . Now move , you are in my way . "

" Excuse me . Let me go hide my head in the ground . "

Reginald made his way out of the kitchen and began muttering profanities when he thought he was out of earshot . Domino glanced over her shoulder and smiled .

" Silly boys . Why do they think acting stupid is charming ? And why am I talking to myself ? "

She shrugged her shoulders and proceeded to fix her self a bowl of soup . As she stood listening to the sound of the microwave fan , she began to day dream of what the future might hold .

Chapter 5

Hill park was named for its benefactor, Montrose Hill, Lily's grandfather. He donated the land and paid to have it landscaped forty years ago in order to celebrate his son Kenneth's birth. It was over forty acres in size with a massive duck pond at it's center. Two lit fountains kept the water fresh and added that extra flair the Hill family is known for. Lily spent many a day here. Her own private kingdom she would call it. The park was there for everyone to enjoy, but they did so knowing who truly ruled there.

Lily was sitting on her bench under the weeping willow near the pond. Her bright green pig tails danced in the wind. She wore neon green contacts, lipstick and short shorts and to set her look, she was barefoot and wearing a black t-shirt saying " *I am the ruler of my universe and all other universes pale in comparison* " written in green lettering. She was very sure of her self for being twenty.

Brad was next to her chatting on the phone. Blond, athletic and blue eyed, he was the classic super boy. Black cargo pants, t-shirt and combat boots attempted to hide the massive muscles beneath.

" Yo Brad. Off the phone. " She pointed to the main entrance. A silver patrol cruiser was making it's way to their location. " Fuck, not today. Seriously ? "

Brad put the phone in his pocket, leaned back and put an arm around Lily. The car came to a stop and deputy Grace Smitter exited the vehicle.

" Always where I can find you. Good girl, I don't feel like playing games today. Get up and empty your pockets, both of you. "

Lily gave her the bird. " Bite me bitch. I am not is the mood for you either so why are you here ruining my Saturday. "

" You listen you little whore, do as I say or your day is going to get a lot worse and what is with the out fit you look like a little fairy "

" Whore ? Out of the mouth of the biggest one there is . I mean seriously . I know you are banging Casidy's dad . I am all about playing but that is seriously disrespectful . I wonder what would happen if his girls found out and as for my out fit , this is a Lily original , girls would kill to get there hands one one of my looks , well those who have any taste at least " She smiled and laid her head on Brad's shoulder .

Grace's face turned red . Her mouth became dry and she struggled to formulate her next words . " How could you know that ? "

" I am Lily Hill bitch , empress of the party , seer of all things . "

" Are you black mailing me ? If you tell the girls it will hurt a lot of people . "

Lily started laughing . " Do you think they are blind . Those girls have eyes and ears . I don't have to tell them any thing . Where do you think I got my info from ? "

Grace lost the will to continue battling with Lily . She made her way back to her car and drove off , not speaking another word .

" I hate her and those like her . You know babe ? "

" Ya . It sucks that Casidy and little Z are going through this crap . I wish we could fix their problems or at least some of them . "

" Fraid it don't work that way . All we can do is be there , you know ? If they need us for any thing they know to ask . It sucks about Sam . I really liked her , not like that prick husband of hers . "

The two of them chilled there awhile . A customer finding them every few, looking for something to make their day more tolerable . Lily loved her ways . She made people happy and got to know who is cool and what they were all about . Her clientele ranged from deviant high school kids to some of Wicker counties wealthiest . She knew every soul in the county , at least by name . Those who weren't her enemies where usually really good friends that would go out of their way for her with a simple phone call .

" I am starved . Lets go grab some food . We will come

back tonight and catch the second shift . "

They got up and made their way to Lily's green convertible . Brad jumped in the drivers seat and started the car . Lily hopped in the other side , looked at Brad and pointed forward .

" To Ray's my good man . "

He put it into drive and headed out of the park , toward their next meal .

Chapter 6

The parish at St . Malachi's was dwarfed in grandeur only by the church itself . A steeple at each corner , they soared to the very pinnacle of the heavens . Made of wood painted white with natural stone trim and accents . It was the envy of most lesser beings .

Victor had been the pastor for over twenty years . Over that time he balanced the will of God with the will of Margret . He feared God but he was terrified of his wife . He was well into his fifties , a few hairs on the rim of is head to remind him he once had a head full . He was wearing black dress pants and an blue button up . The rest of his suit hanging on the back of his chair .

He sat at his desk , reading over scripture , occasionally scribbling notes on a pad . Preparing for his next sermon usually took most of his Saturday . He peered at his notes and began muttering a half done rant. He looked up and paused as if waiting for divine guidance . After a moment he returned to his bible only to be interrupted by a loud knock on the front door .

" I'll get it . " Yelled Margret .

He could here her heavy gait as each foot hit the floor sending vibrations though out the house . " Maybe your voice will scare them off and I can get some work done . They don't hand us money for dull sermons . " He said to him self quietly .

Margret opened the door . A tall muscular man stood before her . His shoulders almost to wide for the door way . He was wearing a white cloak over black pants and shirt . It was trimmed in various symbols unknown to Margret . A symbol of his faith hung from his neck . Behind him a woman wearing the same cloak but over white clothing , blue hair peeking out from her hood .

" Good evening . Is Victor Solomon in ? " The man asked . His voice was bland and his eyes betrayed the fact he knew no kindness .

" Well yes . I am Margret , his wife . Who may I ask is calling ? "

" I am Donovan . This is my aid Tempest . " He gestured to the woman with him . " It is very important we speak with your husband Mrs . Solomon . We are here under the authority of the highest levels of the church .

Margret's eyes lit up . She grabbed him by the sleeve and pulled him into the house . " Please wait here . I will fetch him . Make your self comfortable . " She darted around the corner and banged on Victor's study door .

" Victor . It is representatives from up top . Come quick . "

" Up top ? " He yelled back at her .

" The church dear , they are from the grand church . "

The door flew open . Victor was attempting to put his tie back on , only to get frustrated with it .

" Here , let me . " Margret grabbed it and finished the puzzle , nearly choking him when she tightened it . " Now go . They are waiting for you . "

Victor rounded the corner . Tempest was seated quietly on an antique chair near the front door . Donovan was standing in the same spot Margret left him in . His arms folded , an intense look on his face .

" Welcome , I am Reverend Victor Solomon , what may I do for the two of you ? "

" We have come her on the gravest matter and need you cooperation and hospitality . " Donovan stared straight ahead never making eye contact with either of them . " An abomination to god has made her way here and we intend to end her ways . "

" Are you referring to Samantha Tanor ? " Margret interjected . " That wicked woman found doing ritual magick . She recently took her life . The funeral was this morning . "

Donovan mouth broke into a sarcastic smile . " I have no interest in such trivial matters . What do I care of a foolish woman tampering with foolish things . "

" I apologize . I just assumed . "

" No Mrs . Solomon . The one we hunt is truly dangerous .

If not dealt with , she could bring hell down on all our heads . "

" That sounds very serious . " Victor cringed as he spoke . " Of course we will do any thing to assist you . Please , just ask . "

" You both are true to our ways . Your help will be greatly rewarded in the here after . "

Margret became excitable and grabbed Tempest by the hand , pulling her to her feet . " Come dear . I'll show you where you can freshen up . You must have had a long journey to get here . " She vanished up the stairs , her guest reluctantly being drug behind her .

" I really can't stress the seriousness of all this Victor . " Donovan looked annoyed as he glanced toward the stairs . " This woman we are after is a powerful tool of the Devil . We must end her as soon as possible lest we all fall into depravity . "

" Who is she and how could one person concern you so ? "

" One touch from her brings insanity . It is her way . "

" Her way ? "

" Her infernal power . "

" You mean true magick ? "

Donovan nodded and pulled an exquisite dagger from his cloak . Its blade was slightly curved , polished to a shine . The hilt was ivory , blue glyphs crudely carved into it .

Margret showed Tempest to the bathroom and pushed her in . " You can wash up in here dear . I will fix us all some lunch and you can tell me everything . I decorated it my self . Beautiful is it not ? "

" Yes . Nice job . " Tempest voice was flat and unemotional . " I can tell you nothing . Only Donovan could do such . "

Tempest rolled her sleeves up to wash her hands . Her arms were covered by ropes of blue glyphs twisting around them as they made their way down beneath her shirt . "

" What are those markings on you ? " Margret's voice got quieter .

" My leash . "

Chapter 7

Casidy sat on the rail of her balcony , smoking a joint from the dime she got from Lily before this all started . She held it between her fingers and wrote her mothers name in smoke . " I don't know what to do . There is no one now to help me understand . Why did you let them break you ? Can you even hear what I am saying mom ? " She wiped away a tear and took a long drag . The smoke trickled out of her mouth slowly as if it had no where important to be .

There was a knock on her bedroom door . She put the roach out and put it in her pocket . Wandering back into her room , she shut the balcony door behind her . She opened the door . Persephone was standing there , a drink in one hand and box wrapped in gift paper in the other .

" Nice aroma , you should share . "

" What ? Seriously ? Bad baby sitter . "

Persephone giggled . " Perhaps I am . I will trade you this box for what ever you can spare . " She held it out to Casidy . " It is from your mom , she left it at the library . Well it has your name written on it so it must belong to you . "

Casidy took the box . The paper was blue hearts on a black background . The tag read " *To my sweet Casidy , my most precious treasure* " She started tearing up .

" Um , Thanks . " She reached into her pocket and handed Persephone the roach she had left .

" Cool . I will put this to good use . Get some sleep sweetheart you look like you really need it . "

" Ya ok , I will . "

She shut the door and tore the paper from the box then opened the lid . She reached in and pulled out fine silk .

" This feels nice . She had never given me silk before . "

She pulled out the garment and admired it until she realized what was beneath it in the box .

" What the hell is this for ? Why would mom give me something like this ? I can't take it anymore . This whole thing is driving me crazy . I think I am going to snap . "

She placed her gifts back in the box and closed the lid .
" I need a bath . "
Layer by layer her clothes came off and thrown to the floor as she made her way to the bathroom , panties being flung as she reached the tub . She turned the cold water on and stared at it churning and swirling . Her left hand patted her leg as she waited for the tub to fill . She turned the water off as it reached her desired depth . As her left foot touched the water , here eyes opened wide at the realization of just how cold it was . She took a deep breath and held it as she climbed in and submerged her self . A shiver ran through her as her body tried to adjust to the temperature . The sound of her breath slowed as she listened to it beneath the water . Her eyes closed as she let her head float up for air and with in moments she had drifted off to sleep .

Chapter 8

" Jules , Nick and I are going to play cards in the parlor . Would you like to join us ? " Stacey asked as she bent down to where her young admirer was sitting and kissed her on the cheek .

" Definitely ! Any thing to spend time with you . "

Jules was almost a teenager , her thirteenth birthday only a couple of weeks away . She stood a mere five foot one , her straight brown hair hung to the middle of her back . Her white blouse was tucked into her faded blue jeans , not high fashion for the current times or any other time for that matter .

Stacey blushed at the remark . knowing Jules has a major crush on her made her nervous , flattered and a bit confused on how to act around her .

" Sweet , I like hanging out with you too . "

They made their way to the parlor . At the foot of the stairs sat Nick , eagerly shuffling the cards . They seemed to dance in his hands as if they were happy to be played with .

" Cool , you got Jules to play . " He said as he continued fiddling with the deck . " What game shall we play with three ? "

The girls replied with a blank look as if he had asked them to solve a calculus equation . They sat down before him and stared into his eyes , waiting for him to take charge .

" Geez fine . How about we just play rummy ? "

Nick began dealing the cards to his adorable but easy opponents . He was tall for fifteen , short blond hair mostly covering a scar that ended just above his left eye . A white t-shirt and khaki cargo pants hung loosely on him .

" It's a lot more fun playing with the two of you than Domino , I really hate losing all the time . "

" Are you talking about our intelligence little man ? " Jules growled as she gave began to stare him down .

" Easy Jules , I don't think he meant it like that . " Stacey said as she patted Jules on the shoulder .

" Ya fine , but I'm still taking Nick down . " She picked up her cards . Her soft green eyes peered out from the strands hair covering them and began scanning her hand in the hopes it would tell her how to make Nick eat crow .

Nick quickly realized it was in his best interest to let them win . He figured loosing was far better than having Jules upset with him . He glanced at his hand and shrugged . " Alright , let's play . Jules you go first "

Stacey smiled at the both of them and picked her hand up . She glanced over her shoulder to peer out the door . A momentary shiver took her breath . She shook it of and returned her gaze to her friends .

The sun was near the end of its daily journey . The sky beginning to embrace more reds as the blues began to recede . The shadow of the orphanage began to blanket a young couple leaning against the fence . The young girl began running her hand through her preys hair . Her lips puckering as she leaned in for her quarry .

" Violet be cool . Eric is right over there . " Vander said as he pointed to the bench .

" Relax baby , he is buried in his book and besides all I want is a kiss . " She bent over and flipped on the radio . She began to sway to the industrial beat that emanated , her face betraying the thoughts that raced through her mind .

" *I am all you'll ever need . Falling down to you . To you I can't help but to adore . The both of us wrapped up in the dark . Holding hands , touching lips , feeling flesh , is this sin ? Hey baby show me what is locked inside . Come with me and take a ride . I will open up your mind . Hey baby can you feel your destiny . Find your strength next to me . Our wicked ways the world will see .* "

She embraced Vander and forced a kiss on him . He knew there was no resisting , so he relaxed and returned the favor with passion . His arms went around her and dropped to her waist .

" Lower " She whispered

He complied letting his hands slip to her ass . She came up

on her toes in the excitement , tightening her grip on him . As she began to deepen her kiss , the radio went off .

" Hey what's up you two ? "

Violet released her embrace and spun around . Eric was standing there with a smile on his face . He slowly shook his head .

" Play time is over kids . Go in the house and behave your selves . I will be in shortly . " He turned to the young girl sitting in the dirt . " Alexis you too . "

Alexis skipped toward the house , Ms. Pink dangling from her hand . Violet and Vander quietly followed , leaving Eric to him self . He returned to his bench and picked his book up .

" I need to hurry " he mumbled . " Three more pages , I hope they tell her name before the end . "

" Pandora . " A faint female voice said from behind him .

" I thought I said every one inside the ... "

Eric paused as he realized the voice was not familiar . He turned to see a woman in her early twenties . Her hair was untamed and the deepest red . The look in her green eyes made him uncomfortable . An antiquated black dress with dark wood buttons covered her from her ankles to her neck . Her hands were wrapped in black silk gloves .

She slid the left glove from her hand and slid her finger over his lips . He began to weep and fell to his knees . The tears filled his eyes faster than he could wipe them away . He became unable to move and his vision began to fade . As he watched her walk into the house , his world turned to darkness .

"There you are Reginald . I figured you would be in the attic . "

" Damn Domino I come up here to be alone " swearing as he turned to see she was shaking and had a scared look about her . " What is with you , sorry about yelling at you "

" I have a horrible feeling something bad is about to happen , I feel it in the pit of my stomach . Please I am being serious . "

" Calm down and talk rationally , you aren't making any

sense "

The sound of Violet yelling profanities came from down stairs , followed by Alexis screaming , a piece of furniture being knocked over then silence .

" What the fuck is going on down there ?! Stay here I'll go check it out "

Domino nodded as Reginald made his way out of the attic . She began to sob and could no longer keep any composure . She lightly paced the floor , waiting for him to return and put her at ease . But the feeling in her told her not to get her hopes up . She began to wonder if she should yell out to him . A minute passed and the silence got the best of her . She slowly made her way to the attic door only to freeze at the sight of a red haired woman entering .

" Who are you and what did you do to my family ? "

She barely managed to form the words . Her knees began to fail her as the woman walked closer to her . An bare hand caressed Domino's forehead .

" It's play time little one . "

Chapter 9

Mathew fell out as soon as he found Grace's bed . The last week was nearly his undoing . He couldn't deal with any more grief or self loathing . He just wanted to sleep and for nearly ten hours that is exactly what he did .

The sound of a door opening woke him from his slumber . He rolled onto his back and opened his eyes wearing nothing but a pair of boxers .

" Mathew , I am home . "

" I'm in the bedroom Grace . "

She entered the room and smiled at the gift on her bed .

" Now that's what I want to see when I get home from a hard day . "

" Hard day ? Who are you telling ? "

" Sorry . That little brat Lily got under my skin worse than normal . She knows about the two of us , said she heard it from Casidy . Do you think she really knows ? "

Mathew sat up and shook his head .

" That is all I need . How could she ? Screw it . I am done worry about things . Get those clothes off and come here . "

Grace stripped , letting her uniform fall where it may , and jumped on the bed . She straddled Mathew and began to ride him . She flipped on the radio .

" *Our wicked ways the world will see . Get up off your knees and run as fast as you can . I am right behind you . Our love they shall not ban . We will find a way to their end . We will find a way to become strong . We will find a way to understand . We will find a way to see it all . The key to your door lies with in me . Hold on to my hand for eternity . The world will bow at what they see . For ever and ever I am all you need . Hey baby show me what is locked inside .* "

" I love Nina's Carnival , their music always has grind to it . Do you know what I mean ? "

" Uh huh , what ever gets you off . "

She matched her rhythm to that of the music . Sweat

poured down her as she grew hotter and hotter . Mathew grabbed her by the waste to stabilize her and her bouncing got more intense . A joyous scream come from her mouth as they both climaxed . She ran her fingers through his coal black hair and slid off him .

" I love you . "

" Don't say that Grace . Don't make this complicated . "

" Sorry . It just slipped out . "

Grace had been infatuated with him since she became his deputy five years ago . She saw Sam as the competition and deep down was happy she was gone . Now he was all hers .

Grace's radio went off . Deputy Andy was dispatching emergency crews to the orphanage . Mathew jumped up and grabbed it as the two of them replaced their clothing .

" Andy . This is the sheriff . Grace and I are close . We are on our way there now . Keep me posted on your end . "

" Yes sir . "

" Let's go Grace . "

They exited the house and jumped into Mathew's patrol car . He turned the sirens on and peeled out of the driveway . A feeling of dread overcame Mathew . He knew his night was only going to get worse .

They pulled onto the lot and quickly exited the car . Eric was lying on the ground unconscious . Reginald stood near him facing the flames . His head snapped around at the sound of new arrivals . His blue jeans and t-shirt were singed and covered in ash . He took off running toward the woods screaming " Stay away from me " as he distanced him self from the scene .

" Stop! " Mathew yelled as he began to pursue him . " Grace stay and check on Eric . " Reginald made it to the woods , Mathew slowly gaining on him and with in a couple of minutes both had vanished into the darkness .

Grace made her way to Eric's side and checked to see if he was breathing . As she out her hand in front of his mouth , he began to stir . He slowly sat up holding his head and began taking deep breaths .

" Take it easy . " She laid her hand on his back . " Was there any one inside , the kids ? "

" N.. No , I heard them all run out . I think . My head is a bit cloudy . I still can't think straight . "

" Thank god . I was a bit shaken at the thought of it . Where did they go ? Why did they leave you ? "

" I don't know . Please , I need to regain my senses . "

An ambulance and fire truck pulled up one behind the other , their flashing lights adding to the red glow . As the fire crew jumped from the their truck and began grabbing hose , two medics rushed to the side of Mr . Kaid .

" We will take it from here deputy . " the senior of the two said as he knelt next to him .

" No . I am fine . I just need to stand up . "

Eric slowly began to stand . Grace grabbed his arm to help him up . As he finally got his footing , the second floor of the orphanage fell into the first showering the fire fighters in embers . Yells of profanity came from the group as they made a retreat from the angry monster before them .

Mathew reappeared from the woods and casually made his way back to the scene . He drew a cigarette from his top pocket and a lighter from his jeans . He lit up and took a drag as he reached Grace .

" The kid got away . Lost him at the end of the woods . " He surveyed his surroundings shaking his head . " Eric are you alright ? "

" I don't feel alright sheriff . I don't feel right at all . "

" We need you to come to the station and fill us in on what happened . This is insane and I want to get to the bottom of it . "

" Yes , yes as you say . " He made his way slowly to the car , Grace still holding his arm .

" We need to find those kids and make sure they are safe . Don't you think ? " Grace interjected as she helped Eric into the car .

" Ya , of course . There is one in particular I want to have words with for making me run . " He replied as he made a final scan of his surroundings . " Let's go . " He made his way to the drivers seat and in moments they were off to the police station .

  The fire crew started packing up their gear , knowing there was nothing else that could be done . The flames had died to phantoms of their former selves . A book not far from the bench began to smolder . Ribbons of red slowly ate away at its pages . A title slowly fading as it turn to ash , " *The Touch of Madness* "

Chapter 10

The Hawthorne newspaper is the only paper in Wicker county . Less than a year ago it was the Wicker County Times , owned then by Jeff Humboldt . The paper had made the mistake of running a gossip piece on one Jade Hawthorne , a young entrepreneur from the big city . She made a call to her lawyer and with in a week Jeff Humboldt relinquished the paper in a settlement . She quickly took over and declared her self editor . She had worked hard since then to increase circulation by being thorough , accurate and honest .

Veronica was seated at her desk staring at a blank screen . She began tapping on the side of the keyboard . She sighed and began to type only to hit the back space and return to tapping . With another sigh she reached into her desk drawer a got a rubber band . She pulled her black hair out of her face and and wrapped the rubber band around the excess . She put folded arms on her desk and dropped her head down into them . " Damn it . "

" Whats wrong ? brain fried ? " a man's voice came from behind her .

She quickly rose her head up and quickly spun around in her chair . Micheal the copy editor was standing there hand on chin peering down at her .

" What ? , Just taking a quick breather . "

He glanced over at her blank screen and smiled . " Ya , I see you have been hard at work . Boss lady wants you in her office , pronto "

" What for ? "

He shrugged . " I'm just the messenger . " Micheal began walking off waving to her as he remarked " Good luck . "

Veronica got from her seat and made her way to the editor's door . She took a deep breath and knocked .

" Enter . " A soft but firm voice came from with in .

Veronica opened the door to see Ms . Hawthorne seated behind her desk reading a set of papers in her hand . Her

crimson hair laid loosely on her shoulders . Her green eyes
shielded by expensive square rimmed glasses . She held a
finger up to Veronica as to pause and continued to read .
She laid the papers on her desk and took her glasses off .
She looked at veronica and began studying her young
reporters face .

" Do you know what this is ? " tapping on the papers she
just laid down

Veronica shook her head . " No mam . "

" It is a piece presented to me by a young girl who wanted
a job . It is brilliant and the sole reason I hired her . I wonder
what happened to that spark . "

" Mam ? "

" I am talking about you . " She held up the papers . " This
is a great piece . "

She placed them back on the desk and reached into the
trash pulling out a crumbled up wad of paper and began
flattening them out . She handed the mess to Veronica . "
This is garbage . "

Veronica examined the papers and realized it was her
piece on Sam's death . She shook her head and sighed . " I
don't understand . I worked really hard on this . I thought it
was good . "

" Sure . If she had died of a heart attack or such , it would
have been fine but what happened is huge news and you
down played it . "

" I got all my facts straight . I was trying to be tactful , take
the living into consideration . "

Jade began to laugh . " Oh no you don't . You are a good
reporter . You will not water pieces down so you can be
considerate . That's not your job . You have far too much
potential to throw it away like that . Why are you here ? You
are worth ten times what I would ever hope to be . But here
you are . So either you love the work or you are just bored .
Which is it ? "

" I love the work . Finding the truth and revealing it gives
me a great sense of accomplishment "

" Good . Now get out of my office and go find me

something worth printing . " She pointed at the door as if Veronica needed help finding it .

Veronica forced a smile and nodded as she turned and made her way out , shutting the door behind her . She made her way back o her desk , laid her hand on the back of her chair and paused . " There is no story at this desk Veronica " she told herself as she sighed once again . She pushed the chair under the desk and grabbed her purse . As she turned and began to walk to the exit she saw Micheal get up from his desk and cross his arms as he stared toward the press room . The sound of music flowed from with in .

 " Hey baby . Show me what is locked inside . Come with me and take a ride . I will open up your mind . Hey baby . Can you feel your destiny . Find your strength next to me . Our wicked ways the world will see . Our love will never fade now say it's so . You will beat them all now say it's so . Cast away your fears now say it's so . "

He glanced in Veronica's direction and threw his hands in the air . " Are they serious ? What if Ms. Hawthorn hears that ? She will be seriously ill with them ."

 " Better them than me . I already got one lecture this evening . " She replied as she open the door . " Night Mike . Don't give your self a coronary over it . "

He waved her on and returned his gaze toward the press room , shaking his head in irritation .

She grabbed her keys from her purse as she walked to her car . Pausing briefly to sniff the air . " There is a story out there somewhere " She thought as she continued to her car . She unlocked her door and climbed in . Her black masterpiece of German engineering purred as she turned the key over . She patted the dashboard . " You and I are going places my friend . " She put it into drive and pulled from the parking lot onto the street . She made her way down Kegan and rolled her window down to let some fresh air in . The night air was refreshing and as she continued her drive , she relaxed and sunk into her seat . Her mind began to wander , thinking of a future where she was a star reporter and her name was known world wide . She giggled at the thought . " Seriously Veronica , you can't even find a good story . " She shook her head and sighed . Her police band suddenly came to life . The sound of emergency dispatch calling for emergency crews to come to the orphanage snapped veronica from her day dreaming . " Time to go to work . " She told her self as a smile appeared on her face . She mashed the pedal beneath her right foot harder and the car came to life . She smiled at the thought of finding a good story .

Chapter 11

" Alright Eric , tell me what the hell happened . " Mathew turned onto Corder road and headed to the sheriff's department .

" I can't tell you much sheriff . The kids were all inside . I stayed out trying to finish a book I was reading . When I sat down a woman touched me and my mind became very cloudy . I collapsed , watched her walk into the house and blacked out . I gained brief consciousness in and out for a few . I heard Violet's voice . She shook me and told me to wake up and then Domino's voice yelling at her to run a leave me , that the rest of the kids had already split and then she said burn it . The next thing I remember is Grace kneeling next to me . "

" She dropped you with a touch ? How ? "

" I don't know but it was instant misery . "

" This all makes no sense . We need to find those kids of yours Eric and get to the bottom of this . "

" I won't argue with that sheriff . They are good kids and I love all of them . I ask that you handle this gently though . I am sure they are terrified . "

" Yes . Of course we will . "

They pulled into the parking lot and parked next to the front door . A single white patrol cruiser was keeping vigil in an other wise empty lot . The wind began to blow gently . Some clouds appeared on the horizon , but their weakness was revealed by the bright waxing half moon soaring ahead of them . The fruit trees across the street began to sway in a lazy fashion .

Grace put her hand on her hat as she open the door with the other . Mathew and Eric entered Grace fell in behind them .

" You will sit there with your mouth shut young lady ! " Deputy Andy Bink vigorously shook his finger at the blue haired girl sitting on the bench before him . " I have too much to do to put up with your issues . Your parents will be here shortly to retrieve you . "

" But ..."

" Shut it ! "

He was near six foot high , his uniform laid loosely on his narrow frame . His face was pitted from a bad case of acne in his youth . His hair , cut thin and short , barely appeared from under his hat .

The girl was Heather Paterson . Her features were clearly of french origin . She was barely fifteen , nearly five foot four , slender but firm figure wearing a simple pink t-shirt and blue jeans .

" Please , can I ... "

He raised his hand as if to slap her . " What part of shut up don't you understand little girl .

She flinched and pressed her lips together tightly . The signs of defeat began to draw them selves upon her face . She pulled her knees to her chest and put her head down on them .

" That's better . Now just sit there until your parents get you out of my hair . "

Andy looked toward the front door as it opened . The sheriff had his hand on Eric's back , gently guiding him as they walked toward Mathew's office .

" Sheriff , what's happened at the orphanage ? I heard Grace on the mike . "

" Not now Andy . I don't have time to get in to it . You just man your desk . " He glanced back at Heather as he reached his office . He escorted Eric in and closed the door behind them .

Heather looked amused and began to giggle . She drop her feet back to the floor , leaned forward and put her hands on her knees .

" Somebody isn't the king of the world like he thought he was . "

Andy lunged at her with his hand raised . Grace grabbed him by the wrist and threw his arm down .

" Cut it out Andy . You're not going to hit her so quit acting like it . Sometimes I wonder about you . Go do some paper work and leave her be . You're just antagonizing her and that is childish . "

" What the ... . forget you Grace . You deal with her . I'm going to the little boy's room . " He grabbed a magazine from his desk , stomped to the back cursing under his breath and turned left when he reached the hall , vanishing from sight .

" What a prick . " Heather stood up and bounced about in place .

Grace pointed at her then to the bench . " Park it . "

Chapter 12

Felix had enjoyed his day out so far . After getting bored chasing minnows at the creek he headed to the fish mart and had him a quick snack at the dumpsters . Then he made is way to Hill park and chased some ducks around . He never tried to harm them but he would tag one once in awhile to let them know he could . It was his favorite play spot . His mistress would bring him here often and allow him to run free . After he had enough of the park , he headed down the rail road tracks to find something else to amuse himself with . The sun had set and the sky was full of stars, he saw a figure walking on the tracks coming his direction . He picked up his pace to investigate . It was a girl wearing a white dress with blue plaid trim . He caught up to her side , turned around and headed back the way he came matching her pace .

" Right on time . " she remark as he caught her eye . " I guess we will walk together a few . Yes Felix ? "

Felix looked at her with a puzzled expression . He looked ahead and continued to walk at her side .

" My head is getting clearer . I am starting to understand . Oh , how rude of me . I am Domino . It is nice to meet you Mr. Felix . "

He glanced at her again trying to deduce how she knew his name .

" Ya , I know . It is a little creepy is it not ? It is going to be a crazy night . I know that much . I would not have bothered talking to a cat a couple of days ago , but now I see even you have a part to play . "

She put her fingers to her temples and rubbed . Her head was pounding and the pain was almost unbearable . She had a long night ahead of her and knew the headache was only going to get worse .

Felix stared at her contemplating the words that flowed from her mouth , an understanding of what she was talking about began to sink in . He knew what he had to do .

They came to the crossing at Spire drive . Domino stopped , took a deep breath and looked at Felix .

" Well friend , this is where I get off . I have places to be . You have a busy schedule also it seems . You better hurry on . "

She waved behind her as she walked down the road . Felix looked up into the stars and thought of his mistress . He missed her , but more importantly , he had to do something for her . He darted down the tracks toward home . With in a few minutes he spotted a familiar hill and made his way to it . As he reached the top , he could see his home at the bottom of the hill and across the road . The sun was beginning to rise and illuminate the surroundings . He sat there and pondered what the girl meant until he heard his mistress voice calling for him . His ears perked up and he darted down the hill . As he crossed the road he was hit by a car . He felt his back crush as the tire went over him . Pain shot through him then numbness . The sound of his mistress screaming his name followed by sobbing . He clawed at the road with his front paws pulling him self closer to his yard . Inch at a time , he moved forward until he finally laid in a bed of grass and closed his eyes . A small soft hand caressed his head as a tear fell on his face . With that , he faded away .

Chapter 13

The flames had died under the constant bombardment of water . Small glows of red ran through what remained of the fallen building trying to escape extinction , eating as much as possible before they came to meet their end .

Donovan and Tempest walked up to with in a couple of feet of where the front door once stood . She knelt down and placed her palm flat to the ground . Her eyes closed and her breathing slowed . She started to shiver as the wind began to blow . Her eyes moved rapidly beneath her closed lids . Her hand began to jerk , creating slashes in the the ash and dirt beneath it . Her breathing became quick and shallow . Her shivering turning into trembling . She jumped up and opened her eyes while attempting to gained control over her self . She rocked side to side and began to feel calmer .

" Well ? Was she here ? " Donovan's voice was impatient .

" Yes master and she caused quite a stir . "

" How so ? "

" Children . Nine in number . Their faces twisted as they scattered from this place in all directions . She has touched them . "

A low growl came from deep with in Donovan's chest . He glared in anger at the remains of the orphanage as if to blame it for making a fool of him , then turned his attention to Tempest .

" I am very upset by this . I only intended to hunt her and end her ways . Now I have to add nine more targets to the task at hand . "

Tempest could only nod . Her face revealing her unease at what her master had in mind . " They are only children . " She thought . " They don't deserve what he will do to them when he finds them . "

A firefighter approached the two of them . The words " K Hill " printed across his hat . He was shorter than Donovan but nearly as wide . A pair of sporty safety goggles shielded his eyes . His protective clothing was soaking wet and full of small holes from the embers he caught earlier when the second floor fell in .

" Can I help the two of you . This area is still dangerous . You need to step away from the site . " He waved his hand toward the road .

" We are through here little man . " Donovan didn't bother to look at the new arrival . " We will leave you to your meaningless task . Let's go Tempest . We have a full night before us . "

He turned and walked away from his latest annoyance . Tempest sighed and began to follow him , she looked behind her and mouthed " Sorry " to the fireman . With in moments the two had left K Hill's sight as they made their way down the road .

" What a jerk . "

He walked up to the pile of wet charred wood and looked for any signs that the fire may still be lurking beneath it all . His gaze stopped at a spot toward the back . A puzzled look crossed his face .

" What the ... "

He turned around upon hearing a vehicle pull in close behind him . A black sedan trimmed in silver came to a stop . It's headlights shinning into his eyes causing him to squint . He tossed a hand up in front of his eyes to block some of the light assaulting them . The driver's door opened and Veronica stepped out .

" You trying to blind me girl . Turn those beams off , won't you ? "

Veronica reached in and flipped them off allowing him to once again see his surroundings . She gave him a weak smile .

" Sorry Kenny . " She looked behind him and shook her head . " Was there any one in their ? Please say no . "

" No .Thank god . That fire was extra hot . I can't explain it . It was a pain to put out . It did not act right . Couple of the boys got burnt trying to contain it . Not bad , but enough to ruin their day . "

" What about Eric and the children ? Did any of them get hurt ? "

" Don't think so . From my understanding , the kids split before the fire was started and they left Eric on the ground out like a light . "

" That does not make any sense . I know they adored him . How could they split and leave him lying in harms way ? "

" You got me . I only heard bits and pieces while he was talking to deputy Smitter . What troubles me is what I just spotted in the debris right before you pulled up . "

Veronica's eyes lit up as she licked her lips . " Now you have my attention . Show me . "

Kenny moved to the perimeter of the fallen building and pointed toward the back . Under a few charred boards was a marble statue of a woman near life size . It had broke in half at the waist . Small chunks of stone scattered around it . A foot to it's left was the frame of a crystal chandelier , a handful of crystals still attached .

" What would an expensive statue and chandelier be doing in the orphanage . I am tempted to search the rest . Who knows what I may find in there . I mean weird right ? "

" For sure . " Her eyes were fixed on the crystals dangling from the rounds of metal . " They certainly are in the wrong place . Eric struggled just to keep those kids in clothes and food . This is quickly getting interesting . "

" Is that your word for it . I say more like disturbing . I am all for a little mystery , but this is ridiculous . Super hot fire , kids running off , weird objects in the debris and those two freaks from earlier . "

" Freaks ? "

" Ya . A really big guy with a bigger attitude and some blue haired chick playing in the dirt . "

" What were they doing ? "

" Poking around like you are , I imagine . " He smiled . " But not as cool about as you are girl . "

" Poking around ? Is that what I am doing ? I thought I was talking to a friend . "

" Fair enough . Didn't mean to ruffle your feathers . Look

around all you want . I need to help the crew pack up . It has been a long one . "

" Thanks Kenny . Say hi to Lily for me . "

He rolled his eyes and laughed as he walked toward his crew. " Ya . I'll do that . "

Veronica carefully stepped into the debris , scanning it as she made her way back .

" What is a marble statue and chandelier be doing here ? "

She froze . Something else caught her eyes . Something that turned her curiosity into disbelief .

" A roulette wheel ? "

Chapter 14

Domino made her way down Spire at a brisk pace . Open fields of uncut grass were barely illuminated by the moon slowly making it's way across the sky . She could see a bright sign hovering in the sky just down the road " Ray's Diner 24/7 "

Ray's had recently been renovated into a fifties themed diner . It had a red and white checkerboard decor , a jukebox with all the hits from the era , even true malt shakes for sale .

She made her way inside and sat at the counter . A young man approached her with pad in hand . He was a black man , early twenties with a shinny bald head and a gold front tooth that glittered when he smiled .

" My shift ends pretty soon , but I'll take care of you before I split . What can I get for you young lady ? "

She pondered a moment and stared into his eyes . " Um , coffee to go please . "

" Long night ahead of ya ? "

" You could say that . "

He poured some coffee into a to-go cup and handed it to Domino .

" Cream or sugar ? "

" No . This is fine . Thank you . "

" That will be a dollar forty nine . "

She reached into her pocket , pulled out four ones and handed them to the him . " I need twenty seven cents back please . "

" That's a weird amount , but thanks for the nice tip . "

" Sure . No problem Curtis . "

He looked puzzled for a second then looked down to his name tag . " He-he , I forget my name is hanging from my chest sometimes . " He examined her face and sighed . " Are you alright ? You look a little out of it and aren't you a bit young to be wandering around alone ? "

" Not really , I am out of it and my age is irrelevant . You are getting off soon . Do you think you can give me a ride down the road ? "

" Ah , that's why the nice tip . Ya , sure . I will help you out . It will be my pleasure . "

Domino sipped on her coffee as she watched Curtis finish cleaning his station . He grabbed his jacket and keys then waved Domino to him .

" I ready to split . Where you need to go ? "

Domino got up from from her stool and walked to him . " Which ever direction you are heading is fine . "

" I see . You don't know where you want to be , just away right ? What are you running from ? "

Domino smiled and patted him on the back . " I know where I am going . "

Curtis shrugged his shoulders . " Fine , I give . Let's roll . " He turned and walked out the door , Domino on his heals . He walked up to a red late model sports car and unlocked the doors . He climbed in and started the engine . Domino jumped in the passenger seat .

" Nice car . You must make nice tips often . "

He smiled . " Na . You are my best tipper this week . I have side enterprises , if you know what I mean . This job is a cover so my mama don't ask questions about my money . "

Domino nodded as he pulled out of the parking lot and headed away from his boring day . When they hit open road , he floored it , throwing the two of them deeper into their seats .

" Ya ! I love the rush of going fast . " He glanced over at Domino . " You want me to slow down ? "

Domino turned her gaze from the front window to him . " Huh , um no it's not a problem . " She turned her attention back to the view ahead of her .

" So , what is up with you ? Your a bit odd , cool but odd . You can't be more than fourteen , but you trying to act all grown up . "

" Trying ? " She burst into laughter . " If you only knew my friend . Do you have a knife ? "

" Ya , in the glove box . Help your self . "

She opened it and grabbed the knife . She cut a vertical slit down each side of her dress from waist to bottom , then cut off a strip of blue plaid material .

" Here . Wear this for good luck . "

She tied the strip around his finger .

" I only give good friends a strip of my clothing . Let me out at the next stop sign . "

" It is in the middle of no where . "

" Everywhere is somewhere Curtis . "

" He-he , suit your self . "

They came to a stop at the crossing and Domino got out of the car .

" Thanks for the ride . I will see you later . "

" Sure . Seriously though , where are you going ? "

" To where the moon never sets . " She shut the door and waved at Curtis who took the hint and continued on to his destination . Domino looked left then right . She closed her eyes and images began to manifest , images of possibilities . She open her eyes and turned left . " I am so sorry Stacey " . A tear ran down her face as she headed down yet another dark and silent road .

Chapter 15

The County library was larger than most rural libraries . Two stories high and a basement for archives . The architecture was Gothic influenced , gargoyles perched in defensive positions , pointed arches above every entrance , massive stained glass windows depicting scenes from the works of Homer . It was a mere twelve years old . Built from generous donations from the Arco family . It contained a huge collection of books , a state of the art computer room , a small theater and an apartment , the residence of one Daniel Arco .

Daniel became senior librarian when the building opened its doors at age twenty . He hired Samantha shortly after and the two of them amassed the libraries collection together . His parents died a three years later leaving their wealth to him and his sister who was only thirteen at the time . Daniel was only concerned with the library . He hired private tutors for Veronica and gave her the bulk of the families wealth to do with as she pleased .

Daniel was seated at a desk down stairs peering over an old book . He scratched his head . " Has it been twelve years ? " He glanced at Ivan and sighed . " Why don't you go upstairs and grab some food from the fridge . We will talk after you eat . "

Suddenly the front door opened .

" Hide ! . "

The sound of a book falling to the floor was followed by light footsteps making haste to the back of the library .

Daniel stood up and walked around the shelves between him and the door , relaxing when he saw who it was .

" I figured you would still be up . "

" Veronica , what are you doing here this late . "

" What am I interrupting a date . Is she in your apartment or on the way ? Come on spill it . "

" What . No . I am just really busy and isn't it past your bed time . "

" Very funny . I came here to tell you something really weird is going on tonight . Thought maybe you would have some insight . "

" Weird ? Like how ?

" There was a fire at the orphanage . All the kids ran off and left Eric lying unconscious from my understanding . "

" Well at least they got out . It is a little odd they ran but not enough to go all conspiracy on me . You have been known to exaggerate things from time to time . "

" What !? Are you still ridding me about my theory on what was behind mom and dad's death . I still hold to it . "

" You were twelve and I am just messing with you . "

" Well stop . I have not told you the weird part yet . "

" Go on . "

" I searched the debris . There was an expensive stone statue there along with other things that did not belong . "

" A little weird I guess , but I am sure there is a logical explanation . "

" Ya . Well I am going to get to the bottom of this . Sorry for the late visit . I have an investigation to do . "

She turned and headed out the door . Her brother hit a nerve with his little remark . She has always known there was more to her parents death than a stupid car accident . She also knew her brother kept a lot of secrets from here and she was getting tired of it .

" It is clear now Ivan you can come out . It was just my sister . "

Ivan poked his head around a book shelf , then made his way to Daniel's side , collecting his book as he went .

" Do you trust her ? "

" Of course . I just can't let her get involved , not yet . The way things are going how ever , she will be in the middle of it soon . "

" And me ? What am I supposed to do now ? "

" Nothing for the moment . I have to retrieve some one else in a few then I will need you to do something for me . "

Chapter 16

Scenery screamed past Jules eyes to fast for her to make out anything . The sounds around her rapidly changed and blended with the constant howling in her ears . Nausea set in and her head began to pound . The anguish started to overwhelm her when she came to a stop . She fell to the ground as the world tilted back and forth , gripping her fingers into the dirt so she would not slide off . What little food she had left in her stomach escaped her mouth . She began panting , drool slid from her chin . She tried to calm herself by taking deep breaths and the world started to regain it's balance . After a moments pause , she got to her feet and looked around . She was on a road , dense woods on both sides but it was all faded and unreal . Everything had a lackluster dullness to it . Even the moon in the sky barely emitted any character .

" What is wrong with everything . What is wrong with me ? My head is spinning . "

She started walking down the road , examining her surrounding as she went . It was all so ethereal and dreamlike . She walked to a tree and leaned back to take a pause only to fall through it and hit the ground . She jumped up , a shocked look on her face . She reached for the tree with her hand . It passed through it like a mirage . She slapped her self and yelped .

" Not dreaming or dead . That hurt . Sigh what do I do now ? "

She continued down the road . Every minute or so a gleam of light would catch her eye only to vanish when she turned to get a better look . The further she walked the more depressed she felt . Her stomach growled and she placed her hand on it .

" How am I going to eat if I can't touch anything . "

A loud gargling noise startled her . She snapped her head toward the woods . An astonished look crossed her face at what she saw . It was a caterpillar , a giant one at that . Six

feet in length bright red stripes down a shinny black body .
On top of his head was a circular mouth . It was spitting
water into the air , showering itself in mist . She slowly
walked to it and laid her hand on his head . It was solid ,
smooth and wet . It froze when she touched it , sprayed
water into the air and continued it's way across the road
and into the woods again . She watched it until she lost
sight of it .

" Now I am really confused , where am I ? "

She sat in the middle of the road and rested her chin on
the cups of her hands . Her nausea had gone and her head
was returning to normal . The sound of growling from
below again as if she didn't hear it the first time .

" Quit reminding me . I hope every one is safe . "

She heard distant footsteps coming toward her . She
raised her head to see a familiar face in full color . " Stacey !
" . she jumped to her feet and ran toward her yelling her
name again , but Stacey could not hear her or see her for
that matter . Jules began to cry . " Stacey ! " . the futility of it
sunk in and Jules began to shake .

Stacey was looking around , jumping at every noise . Jules
tried to touch her but the results were the same . Jules
spotted another figure approaching Stacey . A large man
was quietly moving up on her .

" Stacey ! Run Stacey ! "

But Stacey never heard Jules cries .

Chapter 17

Stacey made her way through the cornfields . Stopping only to brush a the occasional bug that got on her . She was covered in sweat , bits of corn husk sticking to her like confetti . The waxing half moon was on the horizon . It gave on a gentle eerie glow barely illuminating her way . She glanced around nervously as she picked up her pace . A snap here , a crunch there and her heart began to race . She could see a road at the end of the tunnel of corn . She made a mad dash for it upon hearing foot steps a ways behind her . She hit the road and sprinted a good couple of minutes until her breath ran out forcing her to slow down . She listened intently but no longer heard her pursuer .

" Your just hearing things . Calm down Stacey . "

She found a comfortable but brisk pace to walk . As she continued to walk the view went from corn fields to deep dark woods . The tall trees blocked the light from the newly risen moon . Her path became darker and she began to shiver . She slowed her pace and reached into her pocket .

" Glad I saved this candy bar I didn't get a chance to cook diner . "

She unwrapped it and took a large bite . She continued to walk as she inhaled the stick of chocolate and almonds . She licked the excess from her lips and fingers .

" We will be ok . "

She saw a light shinning as walked around a bend . It was a house set a little back in the woods . Three older men were sitting on the porch . They each had a can of beer in their hand and were peering into a small television screen .

" Ya ! Did you see that pass . I told you he is the greatest didn't I . "

The three turned their gaze at Stacey as she walked passed them . They began whispering between each other . Stacey picked up her pace once again .

" That's right bitch keep walking . " One of them yelled from behind her .

She broke into a run . She could hear the sound of laughter fading away behind her as she distanced her self . Tears began to run down her face and mixed with the sweat leaving an odd unpleasant taste in her mouth .

" Why is this all happening ? I just want to go home and be with the people I love . "

A deep monotonous voice came from behind her . " How utterly pathetic . To think she would touch the likes of you stupid girl . "

She slowly turned until she was face to face with Donovan . He was holding a long shiny dagger . His eyes cold and hateful . He twisted the dagger between his fingers as he stared at her , the look of disgust on his face .

Stacey could only form one word . " Why ? "

" Because you are an abomination to god , spawn of an evil woman . It is my job to deal with things like you . " In a flash , he slit her throat . She stood for a couple seconds looking into his eyes , then collapsed , falling into a pool of her own blood . Donovan smiled . " One down . "

An ear piercing scream caused him to drop his weapon and cover his ears . It sounded as if it were coming from a thousand different directions . " Murderer ! I'll kill you ! " Jules eyes were intense . She was trembling and digging her nails into the palms of her hands . She began to run at him in a rage screaming like a banshee . He dove for his blade cutting him self as he grabbed it . Glyphs on the hilt began to glow . He jumped to his feet and spun in her direction . " It's over ! "

But Jules had vanished . Blood ran down Donovan's right hand , but he didn't seem to notice . He sheathed the blade and knelt next to the body . He open her shirt , dipped his finger in her blood and wrote *to Pandora* on her stomach .

" That should shake her . Now to the others . "

Chapter 18

A never ending flat wasteland filled the scene . The sun was scorching hot , baking an old woman's skin as she crawled slowly forward . She was covered in rags , blisters on her bare skin , lips dry and cracked . Before her was a tall hill covered in lush grass . She inched her way to it . When she touched its base , she got up and walked . The blisters vanished and she seemed some how renewed . She reached the apex of the hill . A green apple lay on the ground . She bent down and picked it up , quickly bringing it to her mouth . She hesitated , closed her eyes and took a single bite . The sun fell from the sky and darkness covered the land . A hard rain began to fall , drenching the woman and the wasteland below her . She transformed . She had the youth of a teenager . Her eyes were open wide open and a smile graced her face . She looked up to see eight shining stars descend from the sky and dance with the rain drops . The land below came to life as vegetation sprung from the ground . The sounds of animals soon followed . The landscape had become a lush forest . The stars surrounded her and lifted her to the heavens .

Casidy eyes snapped open at the sound of Zia screaming . She became panicked and attempted to exit the tub quickly , but realized her entire body was asleep . She slowly wiggled trying to regain some feeling . " How long did I lay in this tub ? " She finally managed to sit up . Then pulled her self to her feet and climbed out . She held onto the shower curtain until she got her balance then grabbed and towel . She headed to her room drying off as she went . She threw on her jeans and a t-shirt over her still damp body and ran into the living room .

Zia was sitting on the floor holding a blanket . Casidy could see a patch of bluish fur peeking out as well as blood trying to seep through the wrappings . She fell to her knees behind Zia and wrapped her arms around her .

" Of god Z . I am so sorry . "

Persephone was standing with her back to them staring out the bay window . She took a deep breath and sighed . " It has been a rough week for the two of you and for that I am sorry . It seems this is the way of things for the moment . But listen to me well . It will get a lot easier and this week will have less impact on you with time . I love you both dearly and only wish joy for you but that is out of my control . I can only be here for you and that I am ." She turned to face them and smiled . " let's go to the park and bury him . I think he would like that ok Z ? "

" Ya . Thank you . He liked it there . " She got up from the floor being careful with the cargo in her hands and made her way to the door .

" Give me a couple of minutes . I will come with you . " Casidy ran to her room and shut the door reemerging a minute later with shoes on and bag in hand . " I am ready let's go . "

She opened the door for Zia and Persephone and shut it behind her as she exited . As they reached the car she open the passenger door for Z .

" You get in first . " Zia told her as she wiped her eyes .

Casidy climbed in the front seat . Zia got in behind her and sat on her sisters lap . Casidy put her arms around her and kissed her on top of the head .

" I love you so much . Don't ever leave me ok ? "

" Never . I will be at your side till the end of time . " Zia leaned her head back and closed her eyes . Casidy stroked her hair the duration of the trip .

They arrived at the park a few minutes later and drove down toward the pond . Ducks ran to the side of the road , quaking in protest at the noisy piece of metal invading the pacing grounds . They exited the car and began walking to a patch of trees a few yards away . Casidy kept her arm around Zia as they walked . Persephone a few feet in front of them .

" Hey wench , over here . "

The three of them turned their heads to see who was calling who . Lily and Brad were seated on a large stump further away from the pond .

" Go on sis it's cool . Thank you for riding with me . Go have fun . " She kissed Casidy on the cheek and caught up to Persephone , looking back to wave her sister on .

Casidy blew her a kiss and turned in Lily's direction . She raised her hand in the air and waved as she ran to her friends side . She bent down and gave her a kiss on the lips .

" What's up you two ? "

" What's up with you , a little late for a family outing isn't it my pet ? "

" Oh ya . " Casidy looked to the ground and kicked some dirt . " Felix got his by a car . Z wanted to bury him in the park . "

" God , that sucks . What a horrible week . I am so sorry kitten . "

Casidy shrugged . " I don't even have a response to that Lily . "

" No . I guess not . My bad . I would never say anything to make you feel worse . You know that right ? "

Casidy smiled and nodded . " Of course . You are my best friend . "

Lily nodded in return . " Yep . So true . Brad reach in you pocket and light up that sunshine .

Brad reached into his pocket and pulled out a joint . He lit it and passed it on to Casidy who took a long drag and smiled . She handed it to Lily who matched her young friends actions .

Casidy looked behind her but could not see Zia or Persephone . " I wonder wear they buried Felix . "

Brad took his hit and exhaled . " Don't know . Lots of woods that way . I am sure it is a nice spot . "

" Ya , well he is family , so it is cool for him to lay at rest in my park . I'll ask Z later were he is at so I can plant a tree for him . "

" Wow , that is so sweet of you girl . I am sure Zia would love that . " Casidy reached over and hugged Lily who politely pushed her away .

" I love ya girl , but don't mess up the threads unless I get more than a squeeze from you . "

Casidy smiled . " Bad girl . Better be careful , I might surprise you and take you where you sit and let Brad watch us have fun . "

She looked at Casidy with a sense of excitement . " Don't tease me like that , you just got me wet . "

Brad blushed and moved down to the ground taking the puff with him . " I can't handle the two of you when you talk like that . It just ain't right . "

Persephone and Zia came out of the woods and headed to the little party . The joint still burning filled the air with a distinct smell . Zia sniffed as she got close and grinned . Persephone cleared her throat and placed her hand on Lily's head .

" Um , yes . Hello . "

" I am taking Zia home to rest . You will keep an eye on Casidy , yes ? She will be fine hanging with you , right ? "

" Um , yes mam mistress Persephone . I have my eyes on her . "

Persephone smiled and removed her hand . " Good . I am trusting you . " She turned to Casidy . " Have fun , but stay safe sweetheart . "

" Thank you . I need to unwind . "

Zia embraced her sister . " I will see you later , love ya . "

" Back at you cuteness . "

They climbed in the car a drove off . A strange feeling came over Casidy .

" Break out the love darling . I need to relax . "

Chapter 19

Vander and Violet slipped through a hole in the chain link fence and entered Wicker Technology Park , which was truly no more than a bunch of warehouses .

" We will take a break in here . It is shut down for the day so there should be no one around . " Vander held his hand out to Violet .

She grabbed it tight . " Sounds like a plan . Let's rest a few . My head is still spinning . "

They made their way to some grass away from any security lights and sat down . Violets stomach growled in protest to lack of food . She had not eaten since breakfast and her energy was nearly out .

" Are you hungry babe ? "

He could see she was very distressed . She no longer possessed her normal glow and beauty , but looked sad and beaten . It killed him to see her like this . In the eight years he has known her , she has always been radiant . No matter how little she had or how rough life got she always had a smile for him .

" Yes , very . "

" Let us see what I can do about that . "

He stared intently at a large rock . Specks of colored light started to flow across his eyes . He felt a slap on his arm and snapped out of it .

" Ouch . Why did you slap me . "

" What are you doing ? Do you remember the last time you used your way ? You nearly gave me a heart attack . "

" You are over reacting a little . Don't you think ? "

" You opened your eyes and the next thing I see is half the house being turned into a plush gambling room . "

" I was startled and did not understand what was going on . I have a better grip on it now . Don't you trust me ? "

She wrapped her arms around his neck and kissed him on the cheek .

" I'm sorry Vander . I'm hungry and my nerves are shot . Of

course I trust you . You have never failed me . Go on . Finish what you were doing . "

Vander regained his focus . The rock became a mass of tangled lines of colors then transformed into a dinner setting for two , porcelain plates
sterling silverware , crystal champagne glasses .

" Wow babe . You are getting the hang of it . I have to know though . What is it with you and all this extravagant stuff , wouldn't simple settings suffice ? "

" Just the way I think , I guess . "

" Since when . We have never had anything like it . "

" I've been having odd memories . Any ways , on to so food . "

He turned his focus to a patch of grass . Again his subject burst into a tangle of lines . They floated over to the dishes and in a flash , there was food .

Violets eyes lit up as she grabbed her fork and dug in . It was a plate of hot spaghetti and meatballs , a chunk of cheese on the side . Her glass was filled with fresh blackberry juice , Violets favorites .

" This is amazing . You are here by my permanent chef . You don't even have to go to the grocery store . "

" I am glad you like it sweetheart . "

" So sorry I doubted you . "

" You are forgiven . "

Vander smiled , picked up his fork and started on his meal . He watched her eat , delighted in the fact that he was making life a little better for her . Her pitiful demeanor was slowly replaced with an energetic excited aura . The food before her was sheer bliss and satiated her appetite , at least for food .

Vander lost interested in his food as her beauty continued to increase . Her clothing transformed into the hottest out fit Vander could have imagined on her , from her white silk shirt with only two buttons buttoned to the black leather boots that came nearly to her knees . His heart raced as fantasies of what he wanted to do to her floated across his mental landscape .

Violet could some how feel the lust building in him and realized why when she saw her new clothes .

" Sweet . My boy friend is an awesome magickal chef and I can create nice clothes for my self . I am set for life . "

She leaned to him and licked the side of his face . His inner world shattered into a maelstrom of desire . He was nearly in tears .

" Want to play ? "

He got a grip on himself and cleared his head .

" Sweetheart , stop it . You are nearly impossible to resist right now and this is neither the place or time for making out . "

She crossed her arms and pretended to pout .

" Fine . Be that way . But you will have me and it will be soon . "

" That will be incredible but for now we need to get moving . "

He stood up and held his hand out to Violet . As she took it a sense of mild bliss overcame Vander . Just holding her hand was pleasurable .

Chapter 20

Eric stepped out of Mathew's office and made his way to Grace's desk where she was busy doing paperwork . She laid her pen on her desk and looked up at him .

" How do you feel Eric ? "

" I have had better days but I will be fine . "

" We will try to find your charges and get them to safety . What are you going to do about a place for all of you to live ? It sucks about the orphanage . "

" That is the least of my concerns Grace . I just want to make sure they make it to the end of their paths safely . "

" Paths ? "

" As long as they find each other they will be fine . "

" You don't seem very concerned . I figured you would be in a panic . Those kids are probably scared . Any idea why they ran away ? "

Eric paused and contemplated his next words . He knew neither Grace nor Mathew would be able to help them , that they may even harm them .

" I've told the two of you everything I know . I just have a lot of faith in them . They will be fine . They have strong wills and brilliant minds . I am not going to get my self worked up . I will see them all again . "

He patted her on the shoulder and made his way to the exit .

" I will see you in another life . Later . "

" Another life ? "

He smiled and walked out , leaving Grace dumbfounded as to what he meant . What was going on ? Why did she have a sick feeling deep in her core . She decided her imagination was getting the best of her and shook it off .

Mathew made his way out of his office to the coffee machine . Andy had just made a fresh pot and the aroma was a siren's song , luring Mathew to what it offered . He grabbed a large mug and filled it to the rim with coffee .

" Grace . Do you want any ? " He held his cup up .

" Um , no thanks boss . I have had way to much already today . I just want to crash to be honest . I am beat . "

" Sorry . We have a lot on our plate right now . Sleep is out of the question for awhile . "

" Says the man who crashed in my bed for ten hours . "

" I will get you to bed as soon as I can afford to let you go . "

" I know . "

The telephone at dispatch rang . Andy answered it . After a couple minutes of uh huhs he hung up the phone .

" Sheriff the security guard over a Wicker Technology Park says he spotted two kids making their way toward the back of the complex . "

" That is not to far from the orphanage . Grace let's go . Andy man the fort . If you hear anything else , radio me . "

" Yes sir . "

Mathew and Grace made their way to Mathew's patrol cruiser and climbed in . As Mathew started the car , Grace leaned over and kissed him on the cheek .

" For good luck . "

Chapter 21

The Dinomart convenience store was a regular Saturday night stop for Curtis . It was his mom's poker night and if he didn't get her beer there in time he would have to find some where else to live .

It was a one stop shop , an oasis for the late night traveler . Glass faced coolers lined the back wall , filled with a variety of beers and sodas . Racks of snacks and medicines offered their goods , ads for buy one get one free hanging from them .

Curtis made his way to the cooler , grabbed a case of Micky's Lite , his mothers choice of intoxicating liquid then headed down to the sodas . A 20oz Dr . Danger looked like the thing to wet his mouth .

He made his way to the counter , pausing at a glass case full of knives , glass pipes and grinders . He pointed into it .

" How much for the little red pipe ?

The middle aged oriental lady behind the counter glanced at the pipe then back at Curtis .

" For you Mr . Curtis I say five dollars . You a good customer . "

" Sweet , I'll take it . "

She walked around , unlocked the case and grabbed the pipe .

" This one , yes ? "

" Ya . "

She handed it to him , locked the case and returned to her post . He sat the beer and soda on the counter , pipe in pocket .

" Any thing else for you dear ? "

She was surrounded by more sins for sale , smokes in racks behind her , boxes of male growth pills with explicit scenes printed on them , porn magazines in plastic wrap , lottery tickets and even a giant hooka with a sign " You touch you buy " .

" Just a pack of Black's clove cigarettes . "

She placed them on the counter and tallied everything up .
" That will be 26 dollars and 15 cents . "

Curtis handed her the money and took his bag of goodies . " Thanks Ms . Kato . I hope you have a wonderful evening . "

She smiled and nodded . " I will and may you have an interesting night my young friend . "

" I am going to try . Well , I better get home with this beer . Don't want to get beat down . " He started laughing . His gold tooth sparkling from the neon lights .

Chapter 22

A crashing noise woke old man Banor from his drunken sleep . He had just finished his second six pack less than an hour before , so his head was a little woozy . " Somthin messen round with my chickens . "
He rolled out of bed and stumbled to the back door , wearing only his dingy white boxers . He open it and made his way outside .

" Oh for the love of god ! "
Chickens were running every where . One of the breeder pins had been knocked over falling onto the fence , creating an escape route for the now frantic birds .

He walked up and scanned inside the perimeter . Alexis was seated in the corner with her eyes closed , Pink on her lap . She was so very tired and could not resist a nap .

The old man was seriously ill . He jumped over the breach and fell on his face , which made him even angrier . He got to his feet slowly , covered in dirt and chicken droppings .

" God damn it . Wake up you little bitch . "
Alexis opened her eyes and got to her feet , her back pressed into the corner . She clutched Pink in her arms and began to cry .

" I was sleepy . " she said , whimpering .
He reached out and forcefully grabbed her arm , jerking her out of the corner . Pink fell to the ground and Alexis screamed . He drug her out of the pin and headed toward his house .

" Let me go . Please let me go . I don't want to die . Pink ! "
He stopped moving and let go of her arm . " I'm not going to kill you girl . What do you think I am a monster ? I'm just going to call your parents and make em pay fer the damage . Now stop crying . "
Alexis calmed down a little and wiped her eyes . " I don't have any mom or dad . I just want to find my friends . Pink ? " She looked back toward the pin .

" You want your bear ? "

Alexis nodded while wiping her nose on her sleeve .

" Geez , alright I'll get it . You don't move though , hear ? "

He shook his head and made his way back to the pens . As he reached the fence , Alexis screamed . He turned to see what the fuss was , but before he laid eyes on her , Donovan stepped from the shadows and snapped his neck . He turned his attention to Alexis , pulling out his blade as he began walking to her . Alexis turned and began to run , but as he drew closer , she felt her energy slipping from her . He was with in ten feet of her . She was on the ground , panting for air . A wicked smile crossed his face as she began to loose consciousness .

" Get the hell away from her ! " The ground shook with the magnitude of the female voice .

He spun around in time to see the fist of a pink haired woman being planted in his face . He flew back and hit the wall of the house . His impact shattering the wood siding . He got got to his feet , only to be thrown across the yard by his arm , landing on a chicken coupe inside the pin , blade still clutched in his hand . He was dazed and slowly pulled him self out of the wreckage . Tempest was standing at the rear door of the house . She pointed toward the road . Ms . Pink had Alexis on her shoulders and was quickly leaving the scene .

Donovan leaped over the fence and set pursuit . She was running faster than she should be capable of , but Donovan was faster . He slowly gained on her as they made their way down the road . The sounds of a train could be heard in the distance . Pink picked up her speed , Donovan a mere fifty feet behind her . The rail road tracks were now in site , crossing the road ahead . A girl was standing in the road on the other side , her white dress and golden hair a beacon of hope . Pink raced toward her , both Donovan and a train trying to beat her there . As she reached the track , she jumped across , the air from the passing train tickled the bottom of her feet as she cleared its path .

Donovan stopped just short of colliding with the mass of moving metal before him . He began to growl , his face revealing his fury . He ran back a few feet turned and sprinted leaping over the train . On landing he was face to face with Pink . She stood idly with her arms crossed , staring into his eyes . Alexis and Domino were making their way down the road at a rapid pace . He slashed at Pink . The blade slid across her throat yet no blood was drawn . A blank look crossed his face as he watched a smile emerge on hers . She grabbed him by his neck and threw him to the ground followed by a hard stomp to his chest . The air shot out of his lungs causing him to briefly black out .

The train had past and Donovan climbed to his feet . Still a little out of it from the beating he just took .

" How does that little girl posses the Way of Anima ? " He brushed the dirt from his clothes .

" Seems you under estimated the situation master . " Tempest walked across the tracts to his side .

" Where were you ? "

" I neither have your speed nor your strength master . Nor would I have been of any use . Unless you wish to remove these . " She rolled her sleeved down and help up her arms , revealing the bindings woven onto them .

" Don't test me . I am in a foul mood . "

" It is fortunate she is only six . "

" Why do you say that . "

" She is innocent . Some one of age would have tried to kill you . " She shrugged . " Just saying . "

Donovan was not amused , but he had a lot ahead of him and had no time to scold her . He pulled a coin from his pocket and clasped it in his hand . He reached to her with the other .

" Tempest . "

She took his hand . A white fog enveloped them and drifted into the wind , taking them in what ever direction the coin had pointed .

Chapter 23

Every house on Heather's road was near identical . They were a single story high , covered in red brick and had gray shingled roofs . A street light sat on every other lawn , lighting up the monotone surroundings enough to see it was not the place to be .

Heather and her parents , Steven and Emily Patterson , stood on the front porch yelling strong words at one another . Her father had his arms crossed and stamped his feet as he spoke .

" We have had enough of you . You are disobedient , unruly and pig headed . "

" I just want a little breathing room . You chew me out every time I move . It is my life . Now let me live it ! " She turned to storm away .

Her mother grabbed her by the hair . " Enough you are pissing me off . Get your ass in the house now ! "

Heather jerked free . A tuft of her hair still in her mother's hand . She began to cry and rubbed the back of her head . " I hate you . "

" That is it . " Her father open the front door . " Let's go . Leave her out here in the elements . "

Her mother tossed the hair to the ground and headed in , shaking her head and trembling as she entered . Her father followed suit and shut the door . Heather could hear the sound of the lock being turned as the porch light went off .

" Good . I hope you both rot . "

She began to pace in the front yard , tears running down her face , back and forth at the edge near the side walk , stopping to turn around each time she reached a neighbors yard .

" Life is a pain . Is it not ? "

She looked across the street to see a woman coming toward her . She wearing a black cloak , a waxing half moon on the hood . Her face mostly concealed save for her piercing blue eyes and the black lipstick that bordered her devious smile . The cloak was opened in the front , revealing a short black shirt barely covering her breast and a pair of black panties . Her right hand was at her thigh holding a gun . It tapped against her leg in rhythm as she walked .

Heather stopped pacing and began walking backwards away from the stranger . " What do you want ? " her voice meek and frightened .

The stranger aimed the gun at her and pulled the trigger . A dart struck Heather in the leg and her world was instant darkness . The stranger caught her mid fall and drug her to the back yard , out of the light .

She carefully removed all of Heathers clothes and sat them in a pile next to her . She then turned her onto her belly and pulled her up unto her hands and knees . Heather began to stir . Her eyes barely open . A whisper came from her moist lips .

" Why ? "

The stranger bent down , gave her a deep kiss and held her finger to Heather's mouth as to be silent . She watched , unable to move , as the cloaked figure peeled of her panties and walked behind her . She could feel wet flesh press up against her inner thigh , then a hand on her ass . A tingling sensation ran down her spine and her entire body became very relaxed . The stranger gyrated against her . Heather's fear was quickly drowned in a sea of pleasure .

After a couple of minutes the stranger pulled away from her and gently push Heather flat to the ground . As the grass touched her face she fell fast asleep a smile painted on her face .

The stranger returned her panties to their proper spot and knelt over Heather . With black lipstick , she wrote " I release you " on Heather's back . She grabbed Heathers jeans and pulled her cell phone from the pocket . She typed a text then laid the phone on Heather's naked ass .

Chapter 24

" I saw them coming from the fence . " The security guard pointed toward the back of the complex . " They made there way behind Balor's storage . "

" Thank you Mary . You have a sharp eye . "

Mathew pulled the car forward into the park . He slammed the breaks on and pointed at a boy walking from behind Balor's onto the street .

" That is Reginald . "

He tossed the keys to Grace , pulled his gun and headed in Reginald's direction . " Take the car and go around behind him . We will box him in . "

" Got it . "

She climbed in the drivers seat and started the engine . Upon hearing the noise , Reginald began to move at a quicker pace . Mathew ran toward him as Grace took the car around the corner to catch him from behind .

" Don't you make me run ! " Mathew yelled .

But it was of no use . The young man broke into a full run . Mathew set after him .

" Damn it boy . I am too tired for this ! "

Mathew could here foot steps running in the distance behind him . Reginald stopped moving and turned around . His eyes grew wide and anger swept across his face . He started running back toward Mathew . His hands erupted into flames then his entire body .

" What the ... ? "

As he ran , he left a trail of fire behind him , setting the buildings on both sides of the road aflame as he moved pasted them . He screamed and the flames soared into the air . He was an inferno and the sheriff was directly in his path .

" Shoot him ! In the name of god , shoot him ! " Donovan's voice came from behind .

Mathew watched the mass of fire coming at him rapidly . He aimed his revolver at it . " Stop damn it , don't make me shoot you kid . " But the running figure of fire was almost on him . " I am sorry . " He opened fire , unloading his gun at the screaming terror about to engulf him .

The figure exploded . Hot ash and cinders burst into the night sky and began falling . The sight was as if half the stars were tumbling to earth to spend the last of their light in this hollow place .

Mathew brushes the ash off him as Donovan and Tempest caught up to him . His shirt had small holes from flying cinders . His hat laid smoldering a few feet to his left . He shook his head and wiped his brow with his sleeve then holstered his gun . " What the fuck is going on ? Seriously !"

" Calm your self sheriff . You are in one piece and that is all that matters . Yes ? " Donovan crossed his arms and stared at the pile of ash left where the boy last stood . " Tempest . "

He grabbed the hilt of his blade and traced one of the glyphs with his finger . A diamond mark on the back of Tempest neck glowed then faded away . She knelt next to the pile of ash and closed her eyes . Images began to fill her mind .

Reginald came to a stop and turned . It was apparent he had spotted Donovan and Tempest . He stared right through Mathew at the both of them , an expression of desperation on his face . A wave of fire surrounded him . The flames jumped forward , forming a rough copy of it's master . The form charged toward the two of them , the sheriff just an obstacle to be run over . The scene became distorted . She could barely make out a figure stepping from a plume of smoke and grabbing him , pulling him into another plume , vanishing from the scene . Gun shots were fired and ... "

Donovan released his grip on the hilt . Tempest jumped up and trembled as if she had touched a hot wire . She snapped her head around looked at her master .

" You could be a little gentler , you know ? "

" Get over it . Well , what of the boy ? "

She paused a moment and took a couple of deep breaths . Sweat ran down her face as she licked her lips in order to

return some moisture to them . She swatted at an ash
floating in the air .

" He is in the wind . "

Donovan studied her for a moment then sighed . " As you
say . Let's go and if you wine again , the next time I will give
you a real reason to complain . "

" Yes master , I will keep that in mind . "

Donovan turned to walk off , Tempest was quickly on his
heels .

" Wait just a damn minute . " Mathew sounded a bit
annoyed . " You aren't going any where until we have a little
chat . So freeze . "

Donovan turned to face him . He crossed his arms and
tilted his head slightly down to meet Mathews gaze .

" Is that so ? I don't have time to deal with you right now .
Why don't you go bust a whore or something and stay clear
of those orphans . They are dangerous and may very well be
your death . "

" Who the hell do you think you are ? I am the fucking
sheriff here . I will take the both of you in right now for
obstructing justice . You are going to tell me what you know
and now . "

Donovan's hands began to tremble . His eyes narrowed
and he started breathing heavily through his nose . He took
a step toward Mathew only to be stopped by a gentle grab
from Tempest .

" Please calm down master . "

She turned her attention to the sheriff , shaking her head
as she walked closer to him . Her hood fell down and blue
hair flowed around her alabaster face .

" Please . We can solve nothing with hostilities between
us . We do know the way of things , but time is running
out . We must stop the progress of events that Pandora set
into motion and unfortunately , you are not in the position
to deal with the matter at hand . "

" And I suppose you are . That kid created fire from
nothing and then consumed him self in it . I don't care who
you are or what you know , it is my job to protect this

county and I am not backing off . "

Donovan walked up behind Tempest , his finger tapping on his lips . He stared at Mathew a moment then cleared his throat .

" I apologize for my hostility , sheriff . I simply can not afford delays . If you think you need to be in the middle of all this then so be it . Those kids , as you call them , are not the innocent young people they once were . They are abominations , tools of the most wicked of wicked . Do not treat them lightly , for whom ever that woman touches both gains unnatural abilities and insanity to rule them . "

" You mean Pandora ? "

" Yes . I wanted to end her before she caused any mayhem , but I was too late . I feel pity for those she tainted . If we could find them before they do something monstrous , perhaps we can save them . "

Mathew was becoming very tired . He stretched to the sky , then slumped over and sighed . He grabbed a smoke from his pocket and lit it , sighing once more as he blew out his first puff . He looked back toward the burning buildings . Fire trucks could be see coming from the distance . Smoke and ash nearly hid the dying flames .

Grace pulled in next to him and rolled her window down . " Oh my god , what the hell happened . I made the block only to watch it set aflame . I turned around and came back . "

Donovan and Tempest were no where to be seen . Mathew scanned the area to no avail .

" Where did they go ? "

" Who sir ? "

He shook his head and sighed . " Never mind . " He made his way around the cruiser and climbed in the passenger seat . " Just drive . "

" Where ? "

" Away from here . "

Grace put it into drive and made a u-turn , heading away from the disaster area . She laid her hand on his leg and rubbed .

" Are you ok ? "

" I was almost incinerated by a walking bomb , running even . "

" Come again . "

" Not now Grace . I need clear my head . "

Mathews cell phone buzzed in his front right pocket of his jeans . The feel sent a chill down his leg . He dug it out of his pocket .

" God , now what ? "

It was a text sent from Heathers phone . He open it and read .

" I left you a present in Heather's back yard . She tasted divine and fell down so soft . I know you like playing , I do , I do . Consider this gift your first clue . "

Mathew started to laugh and threw his head back against the head rest , crossing his arms behind it .

" Funny joke ? " Grace brushed the side of his face with her hand .

" Ya . My life , my job and this infernal day . I don't think it will end not until I do at least . "

" Don't talk like that . It's not cool . "

" What ever . Turn on the sirens and get to the Patterson's asap . I have a really bad feeling we have fallen into something we can't climb out of . "

Chapter 25

Veronica stopped at the Dairy Swirl to grab her a late night snack , a dark chocolate milkshake . She was getting a little sleepy and needed a sugar rush to get her motivated . As she made her way back to her car , Eric's stepped from the shadows and laid his hand on her shoulder .

" Mr . Kaid , you scared me . "

" I apologize . "

" What are you doing here ? "

" Looking for you . "

" I wanted to talk to you as well , but how did you know where I was ? "

" It is not important . Time is on a leash Veronica . "

She felt as if she was in some kind of spy movie . How did Eric find her ? A chill ran down her spine .

" I saw some strange things at the orphanage . Do you want to elaborate on what is going on ? "

Eric studied her for a moment then handed her the file he was holding . She took it and started to open it . He laid his hand on it .

" Not now . We need to finish our chat . "

She tucked the file under her arm and nodded her head .

" Continue . "

" You have yet to see strange . My shining stars are scattered but they will find their way back together . "

" You seem to know exactly what is going on . It was my understanding you barely told the sheriff anything . "

" You pay attention to details . I like that about you . I always have . "

" We barely know each other . "

Eric smiled and shook his head . He knew her far more about her than she thought .

" Things are never what they appear . Don't ever forget that . "

" If you say so . "

" I only told the sheriff enough to keep him running in

circles . He has no business in this matter . How ever he is now to deep to get out of this intact . "

" Are you saying he is in danger ? "

" Everyone involved is in danger , including you . "

" Me . Why ? "

" Because I know you . You will keep digging until you run into him . "

" Him who ? "

" Donovan . He is an assassin . Pandora and the children are his targets , along with any who stand in his way . "

The thought of someone hunting those kids pissed her off . There is no way she would stand idly by knowing such a thing . It was not her nature . The Arco family has always bravely moved forward when ever they saw good cause .

" How can I help . "

" Just do what you do but do it carefully . I have no desire to loose such a good friend . "

She became even more confused with the friend comment . It was flattering but he didn't know her well enough to call her friend or did he ?

" I can't take it . Why do you keep talking like we are life long buddies ? This is only like the third time we have ever met . "

" If you say so dear . The answer will come to you soon enough . It is time I go . I have a schedule to keep . Be safe sweetheart . "

He walked away and vanished into the dark leaving Veronica with a lot of questions and a mysterious file in in her hands .

Chapter 26

Nick was getting tired of seeing nothing but trees and rocks but Baker's forest was massive , there is no way any one could find him . He had no idea where he was going but he continued forward anyways .

He came to a sudden stop at the sight of a glowing tree before him . He could see a violet aura sweep across it's surface . It swayed back and forth even though there was little wind .

He slowly approached it and saw a carving on the trunk , a heart with the names Samantha and Daniel written in its center . He could feel surges of energy pour from the tree and caress his bare skin . His mind filled with feeling of intense desire and random scenes of passion under the tree flashed before his eyes .

He reached out and touched the carving . The aura intensified immensely . The tree's branches moved in every direction like a thousand arms waving randomly . It began to make a weeping sound .
Rain drops fell from it's leaves as they were thrashed about .

He stood up and backed away . Both fear and awe overcame him . It was as if he woke it up . Was it angry with him ? Should he run ?

The tree calmed down it's tantrum and two phantoms stepped from the trunk . Nick quickly stepped back tripping over a rock . He fell to his back and twisted his knee . Pain shot through his leg as he held back from screaming .

One was male the other female , beyond that the had no discerning details . They floated to Nick . The female reached her hand out to him and help him on his feet .

" Who are the two of you ? "

" We are trapped desires . " Her voice was soft . " The energies of unfulfilled longings . To want so badly yet refrain for the greater good is a lot to bear . Such a thing leaves a resonance . It leaves us , trapped in the lovers favorite tree , their secret spot . "

" Yes and you brought us out in the open , naked and unaware of what purpose we serve . Why were we formed ? Why does one deny his or her cravings ? Who are you to bring us to life ? Those are questions worth answering . " His voice was bitter and strained .

Nick brushed himself off and sighed .

" I don't know the answer to any of them . I just want this night to be over . I want to find my friends , get some food and sleep . But no . I am running through endless forest pausing here and there to talk to tree phantoms . "

" We serve no use here . " The female phantom broke of a small branch from the tree . " We will travel with you and lend you our desires . Use us as you see fit . "

The aura surrounding the tree began to physically consume it . The two phantoms absorbed into the broken branch transforming it into a wand , the names of Samantha and Daniel inscribed on each side a heart on the handle .

Nick picked it up from the ground . He aimed it at himself and felt a rush of sexual desire , the feeling nearly overwhelmed him . He quickly pointed it away then tucked it in his belt .

" Is that my way , unlocking stored energies , utilizing the lore of places and things ? "

He finally started to grasp what he was capable of . The thought of it filled him with a new sense of worth .

Chapter 27

It was the most glorious thing Alexis had ever seen . Several tall towers of steel with blinking lights and dishes covering them all contained in a large fenced in lot . The letters WAXG written in neon floated above a white brick building connected to the fence .

She stared up and smiled . She felt safe here . This place gave her a warm fuzzy feeling in her heart . She twirled round and round her arms stretched out .

" Can we stay here awhile Domino . I like it here . "

" It is just a radio station . Why are you so happy all the sudden ? "

" It just feels right here . "

" What ? " Domino closed her eyes a moment . " Ah . Now I understand . "

" So can we ? "

" If we do we will never see out loved ones again . Is that what you want ? Would you sacrifice them just to stand still ? "

" No ! Never ! Why would you say stuff like that ? "

" I don't have time to be nice Alexis . We can't stay we have to help everyone . I need you to grow up . "

Alexis didn't feel so good anymore . Why was Domino snapping at her ? She adored Domino and trusted her but there was no reason for her to be like that .

" Did I make you mad at me ? "

Domino didn't realize how harsh she was being . Her only thoughts were on what move to make next and keeping her head from exploding . She shook her head .

" No . Of course not . I just need you to understand how serious this all is . We don't have time to play or relax . I promise it will all get better . Alright little bit ? "

" Sure . I will be strong . I don't want to let any one down . I try real hard . "

" Good girl now let's go to the dollar store over there . " She pointed to a small strip mall adjacent to the radio station .

" But they are closed Domino . "

" Good . I need some things and they won't miss them . "

They walked over to the front door of the store . Domino instructed Alexis to have Pink break in .

" Isn't that bad ? "

" I thought you wanted to help . "

Alexis shrugged her shoulders . Pink smashed a large window next to the door and cleared away the excess glass . The three of them climbed into the store .

" Stay here . I will be quick about it . "

Domino darted isle to isle collecting what she need , a can of spray paint , a pad and pen , a candy bar and two sodas . She made it back to the window and the three of them exited .

" Here is something to drink . " She handed Alexis a soda then opened the other one for herself and took a drink . " Ah . Better . "

Domino took the can of spray paint and began writing a message on an unbroken window , then dropped the can on the ground .

" There . Time to move on . "

" Bad Domino , theiven and marking on other peoples stuff . "

" Ya . Bad me . Now put Pink away . "

" But she will protect us . "

" You don't get it do you . Pink is not real . You are the one doing the protecting . She is just an extension of your will . "

" Really . I beat that man up earlier ? "

" You see what she sees don't you ? "

" Ya . I guess I do . "

Pink transformed back into a teddy bear . Alexis picked her up and grabbed Domino's hand .

" Ok let's go find our people . "

Chapter 28

Mathew and Grace arrived at the Patterson's . The lights in the house were off , the only things stirring were some bats out for their evening feast .

" Go knock on the door Grace . I am going to check the back yard . "

" Right . "

Grace made her way to the door and knocked . A voice from with in replied in kind .

" We told you you are staying out side until your attitude goes away . I have no sympathy for you . "

" This is deputy Smitter . Open the door . "

The porch light came on and Mr . Patterson came out the door in his bath robe .

" Officer ? What can I do for you ? "

Mathew made his way to the back yard . Heather was lying on the ground face first . She was stripped of all her clothes , the words " I release you " were written in black on her back . A cell phone laid on her ass .

" What the hell is going on with this . "

He put his hand in front of her mouth to check for breathing then shook her .

" Heather . Heather wake up . "

She opened her eyes . She was filled with a strange but delightful feeling . As she rolled over and sat up , she yawned and stretched .

Heather's parents came around the corner with Grace . A look of horror crossed her mothers face .

" Oh my god ! What are you doing young lady ? "

Heather stood up and brushed the dirt from her belly . She looked at her parents then Mathew .

" I don't know . A girl shot me with something . " She pointed at her leg where a small puncture wound was present . " She drug me back here and did things to me . "

" You mean she raped you ? " Grace's voice was strained .

" Ya . Sort of . She did not hurt me but I was unable to

resist while she had her way with me . "

Her mother stepped to her and wrapped her arms around her neck .

" I am so sorry baby . Please forgive me . We were just trying to teach you a lesson . I didn't know a rapist was running loose . "

Heather pushed her away .

" What ever . I just want a bath . "

" What can you tell us about your attacker Heather ?

She turned to Grace and shrugged . " It was a woman , she was about my height wearing a black cloak and panties . That is about all I remember , my thoughts are blurry from what ever she shot me with . Besides , I am fine . I hardly remember anything . "

" Go in and put some clothes on then come back and talk to me . "

Mathew was finding it hard to focus . She was gorgeous and trying to talk to her as she stood there with all of her glory showing was too much for him to handle .

" Fine . "

She made her way into the house . After a few minutes Mathew started to wonder .

" Mrs . Patterson , will you check on her please . "

She ran into the house only to come back empty handed .

" She is gone . Her window is open . She ran away again . "

Mathew sighed and shook his head .

" Grace . Let's go . Take me to my house so I can grab some things . This night is never going to end . "

Chapter 29

A column of white smoke landed in the parsonage yard. Donovan and Tempest made their way into the house. Margret and Victor were in the living room having a late night cup of tea.

" Ah Mr . Donovan , I am delighted you are back . Please sit and have some tea with us . "

" Just Donovan . You are very kind Margret but we don't have time to socialize . "

Margret looked disappointed . She rarely had interesting guest , let alone ones who were at the pinnacle of the church's hierarchy . She was fascinated by him . He radiated strength and power , Margret's favorite two qualities .

" That is a pity . I would love to chat with you awhile . "

Victor rolled his eyes and glared at her . " Cut it out . They are here on matters of the church . It is late . Why don't you go to bed . "

" Actually , I need to speak to the both of you . " Donovan glanced at Margret and nodded .

" See Victor . I am needed so hush . "

Victor sunk into his chair knowing he was out maneuvered . Every since the two of them arrived , Margret has talked about nothing else . He contemplated finding a motel for his guest and send Margret with them .

" Go on . We are listening . "

" The situation is far worse than I anticipated . Pandora has created a flock of minions . If they are not dealt with , hell will surely be at our feet and soon . "

" Minions ? How many and how do we deal with them ? " Margret's eyes were wide open . The thought of a good old fashion witch hunt stirred the darkest corners of her mind .

" Ten . She tainted Eric Kaid and his charges . They are abominations now , capable of great destruction . "

" You are talking about children not monsters . " The tone of the conversation had Victor in distress . It was one thing to hunt down a supposed demon , but to hunt those kids was not something he was willing to get behind .

" They were children . Their innocence has been tainted by the wickedest of evils . They are lost to us and must be stopped before they bring our end . "

" Have you made any progress ? " Margret ignored her lame husband and his negative attitude . If there were abominations to God running around , she wanted to be part of the solution .

" I managed to kill one so far . I think her name was Stacey . The fire wielding boy is dead as well . "

" Fire wielding ? " Margret was seriously excited . " So they are demons with real power then ? "

" Yes . Exactly . "

Donovan went on to elaborate on the details of his night as Tempest sat quietly in the corner . He told them how he hunted down and killed Stacey , ridding the world of yet another monster as he pulled out his blade and showed them her still wet blood as if it were a trophy . He then told them of his run in with Reginald and how glad he was that such a destructive force had been dealt with . His face was animated and lively . It was apparent how much he enjoyed hunting people .

Margret soaked in every word , becoming more and more enthralled with Donovan and the power that surrounded him . She desperately wanted to be a greater part of all that was going on and Donovan could sense that .

Victor was sick to his stomach . How could he sit in the presence of a murderer . Is this the faith he had spent the last four decades preaching . Did his superiors condone hunting children ?

Chapter 30

Jules was standing on a street , a group of steel towers stood before her . Bright lights adorned them as they emitted waves of colors into the night sky . The moon was ten times it's normal size , it's light illuminating the area around the radio station as if it were day .

A slow sad song began to play from somewhere close . She turned to see a small band , one that took her breath away . Three feline like creatures sat on the ground . They had shinny black skin and long slender tails that were plugged into to an organic keyboard , guitar and mike . Several shining pixies danced in the air around her whispering her name in laughter .

A man with long black hair that covered his face moved his fingers across the keyboard . Melodic sounds came from the creatures mouth .
Jules was mesmerized by the haunting beauty of the music . Another man grabbed the guitar and added his sounds to the song . Jules nearly forgot the misery of the day .

A woman stepped up to the mike . Her was shiny and black like the creature at her feet , shoulder length shock blue hair and illuminated matching blue eyes . Her lips and fingernails were painted hot pink . As she smiled Jules could see a pair of small fangs . Her pink shirt was unbuttoned barely covering her , matching short skirt and leather boots completed her look . On top of her left shoulder sat a blue teddy bear wearing jeans and a shirt reading blue .

" Well well blind man another star fell at our feet . This time she is on our side of things . "

" Who me ? " Jules was in awe .

" Yes you . "

" Who are you mam ? "

" Mam ? Were I come from that is an insult . Are you saying I am old ? How rude . "

" I'm sorry . "

" I'm just messing with you . I am Nina . " She held her

arms out . " And this is my carnival . "

" What do you mean by star . How am I a star . "

Nina stroked Blue's head and contemplated her response . She pointed toward the strip mall .

Jules noticed a sign on a window .

" *Stay on the path . I have faith in you . Love Domino .* "

" Domino . How did she know I would be here ? "

" Seems like she has a grip on her way . You on the other hand seem a bit unstable . "

" That isn't the word I would use for it . I feel so alone . "

" You will get the hang of it . You have no choice . " Nina waved her hand . The music stopped as her carnival vanished . " I understand what it means to be alone . "

" They weren't real ? Please , where am I ? "

Nina shrugged her shoulders . " I wouldn't know where to start . Your path is set as is mine . All we can do is follow this through . "

" So you are part of what is going on ? "

Nina smiled and nodded . " Well I see you are about to leave us , so I ask a favor of you . "

" Um , sure . "

" Tell my daughter I said hi when you see her . I miss her terribly . "

Chapter 31

Zia was seated in Sam's old recliner . It was covered in soft maroon leather , mahogany wood arm rest and trim . A large wooden box at next to it . The foot rest was up and she was sunk into the chair holding a large leather bound tomb in her hands . Her eyes darting back and forth as she absorbed what ever fascinating words it presented to her .

Persephone was seated on the couch , a glass of clear liquid over ice cubes resided in her left hand . She was still in the clothes she wore to the funeral minus the shoes , socks and sunglasses . She took a sip and sat the glass on the end table .

" Well , is it a good read ? "

" Huh ? Oh , ya for sure . " Zia replied , her eyes never leaving the book . " It is very informative . "

Persephone laughed . " Good . I am glad you like it . You are so adorable when you are ignoring me . "

" Uh huh . "

She picked up her glass and took another sip , then stirred the drink with her middle finger . The ice cubes went round and round , each one trying to push it's self to the surface like a game of king on the hill . She took another sip , shrugged her shoulders then downed what remained in the glass .

Headlights lit up the front bay windows . Large shadows crawled across the walls as a car pulled up the drive way . The sound of a car door slamming soon followed as did an inaudible shout .

Casidy jumped out of Lily's convertible.

" Thanks for letting me hang . "

" Sure babe . Your one of my best friends . "

" Back at you . Later Brad . "

" Peace kitten . "

Lily backed out of the driveway as her phone rang .

" Hello ? "

The headlights receded and the shadows reversed their

course as the front door open .

Zia looked away from her book to see who had entered her domain .

" Casidy , yay ! "

Casidy smiled at her little sister and walked toward the recliner . Her hair was wind blown , her eyes glazed over . She giggled as she reached Zia . Throwing her arms around Z's neck , she laid a big kiss on Z's forehead .

" Hello cuteness , what you reading there ? " She tapped on the edge of the book clinched in soft little hands .

" History and stuff . " Zia smiled and kissed Casidy's hand . " you look like you had some fun . "

Casidy stretched and smiled . " I did . I feel a lot better now that I unwound for a few . " She turned to look at Persephone . " Everything good here ? You enjoying that drink ? "

Persephone was starring out the front windows . " Ya , good . " She tipped the glass to her mouth . Vodka flavored melted ice trickled down her throat . " He is home . "

Another set of headlight stirred the shadows into action . They made their way to the other side but vanished this time as the headlights turned off . After a moment , Mathew entered .

" Hey girls . I'm not staying . I just need to grab some things . It has been a crazy night . "

He walked toward his study , stopping as he neared Casidy . He sniffed the air around her and got very agitated . He grabbed her by the arm and pulled her to him .

" Why do I smell marijuana on you . Have you been hanging out with Lily . " He shook her . " Answer me Casidy Tanor . "

She jerked away from him and stomped the floor . " My name is Casidy Rain . "

He drew his hand back and slapped her across the face . She let out a cry and fell to her knees covering the side of her face with her hand .   Zia dropped her book and leaped over the arm of her chair . Two steps and she was at her sisters side . She laid her hand on Casidy's head and glared at her father . The look in her eyes lethal with a sense of finality .

 " If you ever touch her again , you had better not sleep with your door unlocked or in this house for that matter . " She was breathing heavily . Tears vibrated down her face as she shook uncontrollably .

Mathew contemplated turning his wrath toward Zia , but he could see she was angry enough to be serious . He stepped back as a feeling of dread crept into him as he looked into her eyes .

 " I don't have time for this . The world is falling apart outside . I will deal with the two of you later . "

Mathew glanced at Persephone . She was peering into her empty glass as if oblivious to what just transpired . He turned and went out the door , slamming it behind him . Headlights again set the shadows into motion , yet they seemed less eager this time .

 " Sis , are you ok ? " Zia ran her fingers through Casidy's hair . " I meant what I said . He better never hit you again . "

 " I know . " her voice was quiet and monotone . " I know you would . Just don't think like that . You are way to sweet to think like that . "

She wrapped her arms around Z's waist and squeezed . " I love you too much to wish such a thing . "

Casidy got up a headed for the front door . She paused as she opened it and looked back . " Don't ever change . You are perfect . "

She continued on , softly shutting the door behind her . With in a minute the sounds of a motorcycle starting could be heard .

 " She is taking dad's bike . " Zia glanced at Persephone .

 " Do you want to stop her ? It is on you . " She ran her finger around the bottom of the glass then placed it in her mouth .

 " No . No way " Zia replied as she sat back in her seat and picked up her book . " I have faith in her . "

Chapter 32

Reginald stomach was a little queasy . Traveling via puffs of smoke is a fast shaky ride . His right hand was full of Daniel's shirt sleeve , his left was balled into a fist , finger nails nearly piercing his skin .

" You can let go now . Ride is over . "

Reginald relaxed and let go of Daniel . He closed his eyes and took a couple of deep breaths to return his world to normal . Well as normal as it will ever be .

" Reginald ! " Ivan was very happy to see his friend . " Are you ok ? "

" Ya man . My clothes are a little singed , my head is spinning and I am still in disbelief as to what I just did , but other than that I am fine . How about you ? Are you hanging in there ? "

" I guess . I am really glad to see one of you . Is everyone else ok ? "

" Don't know . You are the first one I have seen since we ran . I was on Vander and Violet's trail , but I got boxed by the sheriff and that creep that is hunting us . "

" You mean Donovan , right ? " Daniel's voice was irritated .

" Is that his name ? Do you know him ? "

" Not directly Reginald . He murdered my parents and some friends of mine about nine years ago . He is like a machine . He won't stop until he finishes his task or get's destroyed . The later is my preference . "

" I tried to fry him but the sheriff was between us . I didn't think it would be right of me to kill him . He is innocent in all this . Right ? "

" I am a little biased so I will refrain from answering that . As to Donovan , it will take more than fire to end him . He is immune to most attacks and he wields a blade of bindings , making him very dangerous . "

" Blade of bindings ? "

" It allows him to drain the energy from emergents and wrap them in bindings , preventing them from utilizing their ways . Keep your distance from him , better yet , avoid him altogether . "

" Some one needs to deal with him , right ? "

" Look Reginald , you have a lot of power at your finger tips , more than you know but you have to choose your battles wisely . This is only the beginning . Donovan is just one man . His superiors have ample minions to replace him and most are tougher than he is . They will not quit . When they realize what is truly going on , he will be the least of our worries . "

" More will come ? "

" Count on it . "

" Why did the lady wait till now to wake us up . If you all knew this was going to happen , would it have been better to get us ready earlier ? Why keep us in the dark so long ? "

" You all ? Who is you all ? "

" I don't no man . Why you messing with me ? Who ever set all this up . Who ever decided that thing were to play out this way . "

" Ah , her . Sorry Reginald , I only know so much myself and what I do know I can only tell you according to my script . Any deviation could ruin the entire plan . We all just have to play our part as it comes to us . Besides you know her better than I do ."

" Her who ? "

" Your friend Domino . Everything will play out according to her choices . Only she knows the way to finish what was started nine years ago . She is the path . "

" Domino ? Wow , as if her head wasn't big enough already . Wait . What did you start nine years ago ? "

" To free the world from the Veil and defeat it's architect's "

" The Veil ? "

" For now , let's just say it prevents people from being their true total selves . It blinds them , prevents them from seeing the true reality that surrounds them . It is the great lie . "

" So we are being hunted because we broke through . "

" They fear anyone with open ways who are not under their control . If you were to demonstrate what you are capable to those who are asleep , it would open their eyes . They would start to doubt a lifetime of conditioning , a life time of thinking such things are impossible . "

" They fear us because we can start to wake up those around us and that would be the end of their four century reign over earth . " Ivan was tired of listening . He wanted to show off what he had already learned . " It is up to us to bring the Veil down , person by person if that is what it takes . "

" Wow , listen to braniac over there . You seem to know your place in things . That's cool . I will let you know when I figure mine . "

Daniel made his way to a reading table and sat down then waved Ivan over to him .

" Sit down . I need to see exactly what happened at the orphanage . Show me Ivan . "

Ivan sat down and closed his eyes . He reached out and touched Daniel's for head with a finger . The library faded from Daniel's view . Images and sounds from the incident began to fill his mind .

Chapter 33

Eric fell to his knees as Pandora made her way to the door . She paused and looked over her shoulder .

" I look forward to meeting the real you my love . "

Violet came around the corner to see Eric on the ground outside and Pandora entering her home . She held up a finger and pointed in at Pandora .

" What did you do to Eric you bitch ? Get the hell out of our house ! "

Pandora stoked the side of Violet's face with her bare hand and caught her as she fell to the floor unconscious .

Vander leaped at Pandora but she merely grabbed his arm and tossed him to the couch . He was out when he hit it , his impact knocking it over .

She glanced at Ivan , who had been standing there silently watching .

" Oops . Sometimes I forget my own strength . "

Alexis screamed and started to run as Jules , Nick and Stacey started to get to their feet but to no avail . Pandora closed her eyes and exhaled . Several small red orbs of light with black smoke tails shot from her mouth . In an instant all but Ivan went out like a light .

Pandora leaped to Ivan and touched him on the nose and smiled . She then quickly made her way to the side of the stairs in time to grab Reginald's hand before he saw her . She moved around and caught him , gently laying him on the floor . She waved for Ivan to follow her and headed up the stairs .

Domino was on her way to investigate , when Pandora entered the attic , Ivan behind her . She was scared but mustered the will to ask Pandora what she did to her family .

Pandora stroked Domino's forehead .

" Play time little one . "

Memories forgotten flooded into Domino's mind . Her head began to spin as tears poured down her face . Her world was turned upside down in a brief moment .

" I am sorry for this Domino . Only you can save them . You have to finish what you started . I know it is a lot to bear . We all have faith in you . Do you have faith in yourself is the question . "

" Yes . I won't fail . I understand my path . "

" Good . We will meet again , I'm sure . Good luck . "

A puff of black smoke enveloped Pandora then vanished . Domino headed down the stairs , Ivan quietly followed clenching his book in his hands .

Violet was awake holding her head . She slowly made her way to her feet as Domino and Ivan hit the bottom of the stairs . Vander jumped up and screamed . Half the interior of the bottom floor along with most of the furnishings turned into millions of colored lines . It sounded like a massive swarm of flying insects . Jules woke up to the spectacle as did Alexis . They both panicked at the sight . Jules simply disappeared from where she lay . Alexis clutched Pink in her arms and blacked out again . Pink transformed , grabbed her and ran out the door .

The lines settled and the room was now a luxurious private gambling room completer with a grand roulette wheel . Vander fell to his knees and grabbed his head . Violet grabbed him and pulled him out side next to Eric .

Stacey and Nick awoke next . They stood up and looked around them to see what was going on . Neither had ever seen such a beautiful room , not that they could remember any ways .

" You two split up and run . He is close . Now go ! " Domino pointed out the door .

The two of them did as they were told , somehow knowing that Domino knew what she was doing . The ran out the door then off in different directions .

Reginald was the last to rise . Domino took his hand and pulled him out the door .

" Let's go Ivan . "

Ivan was lost in the detail of the room . How did Vander do that ? It was the coolest thing Ivan had ever seen , even in the books he read . He shook free of his awe and made his way outside .

Domino put her hand on Violets shoulder .

" Leave him be . He doesn't need our help . Take Vander and run . "

Violet grabbed Vander's hand and headed across the street and over the tracks .

Domino knelt next to Eric . She took his cell phone from his pocket then his wallet . She opened the wallet and took the money out then threw the wallet on the ground .

" Four dollars . Reginald , burn it down . Wait for the sheriff to arrive then run . Ivan follow Orion's belt until some one retrieves you . I love you both . Be careful . "

She crossed the street then ran down the tracks .

Reginald held his palms facing the house . They ignited into flames , the house quickly followed . With in seconds the orphanage was covered in flames .

" You heard Domino . Orion's belt . Now go . "

Chapter 34

A red crotch rocket pulled into the parking lot at Ray's . Casidy climbed of the bike and put her helmet away . She made her way into the diner and looked around for a good seat . She spotted Kenny and made her way to him while waving .

" Hey papa K ! What has been going on with you ? " She sat in the booth across from him .

" What's up sweety ? Every thing good with you ? "

She stared at the neon lights above her and shook her head . " I don't know yet . My mind is racing . I haven't been right for a few days now . I thought mom's funeral would give me some closure but it only pushed me further into confusion . " She smiled and shrugged her shoulders . " But what can you do ? Right ? "

" You know you can talk to me about any thing . You are Lily's best friend and I love you like my own . "

" I know . I am very happy that Lily has such an awesome dad . "

Kenny blushed . He knew Casidy practically all her life . He also knew she was putting on a front . She was way too chipper considering what she had been through .

" You are sweet , little girl . I understand there is a lot of friction between you and your father right now but I am sure he loves you . If you don't talk to him , you will never be able to mend your family . "

Casidy lost her smile . Her casual demeanor turned serious as she stared into Kenny's eyes .

" No . It will never happen . I know you mean well but there is nothing that can be done to fix what he broke . He drove mom away . He has no concern for any one but himself . I don't want mend anything concerning him . I am sorry to say this but I despise him . "

" Wow . That is pretty harsh . I don't know how to respond to that . "

Kenny contemplated how lucky he was to have such a close

relationship with Lily . If she had ever said things like that about him , it would destroy him . He knew it was time to change the subject .

" Are you hungry ? Order what ever you want , my treat . "

Casidy's smile returned as she picked up a menu . " I like the word anything . Now what is the most expensive meal on here . "

Kenny started laughing . " Ouch . You are almost as brutal as Lily . "

" Just teasing . Sorry about going all weird on you . I am glad I have people who care enough to listen to me . You and Lily will always be family to me . I trust both of you and I love both of you . So how about you ? How are you doing ? "

" Nothing to complain about . It was an interesting night how ever . That fire at the orphanage was like nothing I had ever seen before . That house burn down so fast , there was no saving it . I have never seen a fire that hot before . "

" Orphanage ? Was any one hurt ? "

" A couple of my men got sprayed by hot embers but there injuries were minor . There was no one in the house which was a huge relief . "

" That's good . Order me a burger a fries please . I need to use the little girls room . I will be right back . "

She got up from her booth and made her way to the back of the diner . Kenny flagged the server down and ordered Casidy's meal . He was glad he could do something for her , even if it was just a burger and a chat .

Chapter 35

Veronica had just finished reading the file . She arrived at the paper over half an hour earlier but was still in her car . After reading it's contents , she knew the matter was to big to ever write a story on .

" He is right in the middle of all this . I am going to kill Daniel . Keeping this kind of secret from me is unforgivable . I knew mom and dad did not die in a plane crash . That girl and her plan , why am I being told now . "

There was a sharp tap on her window . She snapped her head up to see who it was . Tempest was waving at her .

Veronica closed the file and stepped from her car . She was getting a little tired of people popping in on her in dark places .

" Yes . Can I help you ? "

" Sorry to bother you . Do you work here ? "

" Um , yes . I am a reporter . Why do you ask ? "

" My master would like a word with you then . " She pointed at Donovan who was a few feet from them standing in the shadows .

" Um , this is a little creepy . "

" Quit messing around Tempest . " Donovan walked up to the two of them . " Forgive my assistant . She is over dramatic sometimes . My name is Donovan and yours . "

Fear shot through Veronica's mind . The assassin Eric mentioned and the details of some of his atrocities in the file . She clenched the file in her hands .

" Veronica . "

It was apparent in her voice how frightened she was . Donovan knew she somehow recognized him .

" Is there a problem , Veronica ? "

" N..No why ? "

" You look a little pale . What is in that file you are so fond of ? "

" R..Research for a story I am working on . "

" Ah . What does it concern ? "

" A woman that committed suicide . "

" The Tanor woman , yes ? "

" Right . "

She was panicked . She had to calm down if she was going to get out of this , but she had never been this scared before . She started slowly backing away from Donovan .

" Are you going some where ? "

" What do you want ? "

" Oh that , of course . I am looking for Jade Hawthorne . I am an acquaintance of her sister Pandora . Do you know if she is here ? "

Veronica's fear turned to curiosity . What did Jade have to do with any of this ? Better question , why was a murderer inquiring about her ? Is any one she knows safe ?

" No , not at this hour . She is probably at home getting her beauty sleep . She needs it . "

Donovan was a little puzzled . She was terrified but her demeanor quickly changed . He moved toward her , causing her to jump back , trip and fall into a puddle of water .

" Hey ! Get the hell away from her ! " Lily waved her fist at him as her and brad ran to Veronica's side . " Did he push you ? "

" No , no . We were just talking and I tripped . "

Brad helped her onto her feet . Lily's eye's remained fixed on Donovan , ready to pounce if he gave her cause .

" I was just asking her if she knew were to find someone . Thank you for your time , Veronica . Let's go Tempest . "

Lily watched the two of them until she lost sight of them .

" You are soaked Veronica . Babe grab her something to change into , find something cute . "

Brad ran back to the car and opened the trunk . A couple of minutes later he returned with some jeans and a t-shirt and handed them to Veronica .

" Get changed . Brad turn around and give her some privacy . "

Brad complied and Veronica changed her clothes .

" You two stay here please . I need to go in and get Jade . She is in grave danger . "

Chapter 36

Persephone lit up the roach she had gotten from Casidy. As she exhaled her first drag, she sighed. " If only this would cure my woes. Hell, I will be happy if I even feel it's effects. " She glanced at Zia. " So are you making any progress ? "

Zia continued to peer into the book on her lap. Her eyes danced across it's pages with a sense of wonder. " It is all fascinating. I think I have a pretty good understanding of the basics. "

" You need more than the basics. I know this is a lot to deal with but time is on a leash little bit. "

" Don't worry. I will be ready. It is more like refreshing my memory than learning something new. It is weird how familiar all this is. "

" That is curious. This is the first time I have ever delved into this realm of things. I will follow your lead for awhile. You seem to be a natural my little butterfly. "

Zia's heart raced in anticipation of getting to use her new found knowledge. The large leather tomb felt like an old friend telling her all it's deepest secrets, showing her the way toward self completion. She was enamored at the thought of what she could do. Her patience was beginning to waiver. She was ready to use what she had learned.

" I am really excited about all this. It is going to be incredible. " She looked up from the book. Her eyes dropped and a sad look crossed her face. " It really sucks that we couldn't tell Casidy what is going on. Do you think she will forgive me ? "

Persephone inhaled the rest of the roach and blew out a huge plume of smoke. It hovered in the air and slowly came together to form the shape of a heart, then she blew it away. " Sweet thing, You are her treasure. If she wants to get angry at some one, she can aim it at me. I am far more to blame for all this than you. Besides, all you have to do is give her one of your sad looks and she will melt. " She

licked her lips and smiled . " Everything will work out .
Casidy adores you . She will understand why you had to
keep secrets from her . I know . "

" I still don't feel good about it . I understand why it is
necessary but she is the one person I never want to hide
from . I want to be at her side for ever . I couldn't imagine
my life with out her . "

" The two of you are very lucky to have each other . "
Persephone closed her eyes and sighed . " Having a sister
that loves you as much as she does is an amazing gift .
Blood is not enough to form a bond like the one between
you and Casidy . The two of you are connected at the core .
I envy both of you . "

" I have known you for awhile but I don't know a lot about
you . Do you have any family ? "

Persephone pondered Zia's question . The word family was
hard for her to grasp . It brought back memories she wasn't
ready to deal with . She took and deep breath to center
herself .

" Define family . "

" Um . You know , bothers , sisters , people like that . "

" You always have to be clever , don't you ? I have a sister
and a cousin . We are the last of our lineage , but I don't
consider my sister as family . "

" Why ? Don't you love each other ? "

" No . She betrayed me along time ago and cost me a
great deal . "

" I'm sorry . That sucks . Will you ever forgive her ? "

" Not in this life time . "

" I could never imagine Casidy and I being like that . I am
very lucky to have her . What about your cousin ? "

" She has had it pretty rough . She lost everything dear to
her as well , including her daughter . This whole thing has
cost so much . Too many people have suffered just so a
hand full of pricks could maintain their control . I am eager
to see the end of it all and I am very happy you are along
for the ride . "

" Well , Casidy and I are your family . I hope you know

that . I am a little anxious about what is going to happen but I trust you when you say it will all work out . "

" Now that I think about it , I have a pretty big family . I love and am loved by a lot of people . I have touched so many lives . It will be glorious when I can be with all of them as my self . I am tired of putting on mask . The time for secrets is coming to a close and I am over joyed about that . "

Chapter 37

" I screwed up Grace . My self pity is going to cost me everything . I should never have slapped Casidy . "

" From what you said she had it coming . "

" No . We just put their mother in the earth and I never even thought about the two of them . All I wanted was to curl up and hide from them . I can't seem to deal with this week . "

" Do you think you are hiding from your girls ? Why would you do that ? I think you are good father to them . "

Mathew knew to the contrary . He practically pushed Sam off that bridge . After her little secret became public , he treated her like dirt as the girls watched , unable to do anything about it . Casidy blamed him . He did not doubt that fact . He was only concerned with himself and he knew that .

" I am a lousy father . I didn't even have the strength to swallow my own demons and pay attention to how they must be feeling . Besides you did not see the look on Zia's face . She threatened my life , my little girl . I truly think she meant what she said . Casidy is her treasure and I crossed the line . "

" You let her get away with threatening you ? That kind of thing deserves a swift response . "

" No . Zia has never been anything but the sweetest girl . For her to say what she did only means I messed up bad . "

Grace leaned across the console and kissed him on the cheek . She did not want to hear him talking like that . She just wanted his lips and his attention . He pushed her away and shook his head .

" No more Grace . I have messed up enough . I can't be with you any more . I need to put my family back together again if I can . Casidy and Zia deserve better than I have given them . It is time for me to be a man and start thinking about my girls . "

Grace felt a sharp pain in her heart . Was he telling her

they were through ? She wanted him more than anything and to loose him would be her demise . A mixture of sorrow and rage shot through her . If he no longer wanted to be with her , what was the point in her life ?

" What are you saying ? Are you going to toss me to the side because you suddenly feel bad about us ? I have given you all of me . You can't just toss me away like I was nothing ! What will I do with out you ? "

" What ? I didn't mean it like that . Let's just chill out . My head is too cloudy to think straight , alright ? We will figure it out . "

" Fine . I get it . "

Mathews cell phone rang . He slid it from his pocket and looked to see who was calling on him .

" Victor ? "

He answered the phone .

" It is a little late for a spiritual talk isn't it Victor ? "

" *Mathew , I am ...* "

" Are you ok ? "

" *No . I am standing next to a dead girl .* "

" What are you talking about ? "

" *Stacey from the orphanage . Her throat has been cut and I feel I am partially to blame . Mathew , you need to come pick me up . We need to talk . I am afraid of what else may happen . I don't know what to do next . I am lost .* "

" I have never heard you talk that way Victor . I didn't think anything could shake you . "

" *Please just come get me . I am seriously scared .* "

" Tell me where you are Victor . We are on the way . "

Chapter 38

" *These words I lay before me are my last . Then pen I hold , the last voice I have . My world is bleak and boring . It is bereft of meaning . No color flows past my eyes . I sit alone day after day wishing for something wonderful to happen in my life , a spark of something new and beautiful , one moment of joy or bliss to show me life is worth something . Nothing satiates me . I am trapped in a cage of meritocracy and the mundane . Where is the fantasy , the thrill , the sense of awe ? Not in my life . Death is my only salvation . Good Bye to any concerned .*

Lilith rolled the paper up and placed it on her pillow . This was her third suicide attempt with in a year . The first two failed due to outside intervention . Her father stopped her the first time . He walked in on her as she was raising his 9mm to her head . The second was her visiting cousin . He found her moments after she sliced her wrist open vertically down the vein . She had full intention of dying on both occasions and on this night she was going to succeed . Her parents were gone for the evening . There was no one to stop her this time .

She climbed up on her bed and and looked around her room at the sad reminders of her eternal boredom , a poster of Nina's Carnival on her wall , a stack of video games on the book shelf along with a collection of horror novels , a half finished jigsaw puzzle of the lunar surface . No matter what she tried to amuse herself with , it never made her happy , barely entertained at best .

She grabbed a the bottle of pills she had stolen from her mothers medicine cabinet of her nightstand and read the label . " *Take one pill before bed time . Warning will cause drowsiness . Side effects are ...* "

"Side effects , heh . I just care about the drowsiness . Well good bye world , I'm sure you will get along fine with out me . "

She opened the cap and poured the contents into her

cupped hand .

" There is a better way . "

The voice startled her . She sprung to her feet , pills flying in every direction , her note falling to the feet of a woman wearing a cloak , standing in her bedroom door .

She bent down , picked it up and began reading . Lilith walked off the bed toward her . A look of curiosity filled her eyes as she stared at her guest .

" Who are you ? " Inquired Lilith .

The woman held her finger up and finished reading the note .

" I am your freedom from misery . "

She laid a tranquilizer gun on Lilith's dresser .

" I don't think I'll need that . "

" Where you going to put me out ? Why ? "

" There is something I need to do to you . "

" Do what ?"

" Unlock the energies trapped inside you . "

" Energies ? What are you talking about ? Just kill me . That will solve my problem . "

" I am not going to kill you . There is too much for you to live for . I can release you from what binds you . Were you not waiting for something wonderful to happen to you , something beyond the mundane ? Death is not the answer . You have to chase your bliss to find true salvation from misery . "

" I have no bliss , that is the problem . "

" Nonsense . We all have bliss locked inside us . We are just blind to it because of social conditioning , being told that we are not worthy of joy , that we are small and unimportant . You live in a mundane world because that is all you choose to see . Let me show you there is more . Let me make love to you and open your eyes . "

" Who are you ? "

She pulled her hood of her head and blew Lilith a kiss .

" You ! What is with the outfit ? Better question , what is up with you trying to seduce me ? Does this have anything to do with your .. "

The woman placed a finger on Lilith's lip .
" Trust me . "
Lilith was ready to die but decided one more failed attempt could be added to her streak . Maybe her guest had the key to her joy . Could she have the key to Lilith's need , the need to feel excited and alive , only one way to find out .
" Why not . Alright , show me a reason to live . "
The woman took her cloak off and tossed it to the floor . Her panties and shirt followed suit . She softly pushed Lilith onto the bed and climbed on next to her . She took her time removing Lilith's clothing , pausing to kiss and lick each spot of newly revealed flesh . Lilith felt a surge of energy with each kiss . Shivers of new sensations raced through her . As the woman made her way down , Lilith felt an explosion of energy washed over her . Her breathing became deep and heavy . Her entire being tingled with delight . A longing for life seeped into her mind . A wave of pleasure washed over her . After a few minutes the woman climbed up her and delivered an amazing kiss to Lilith's lips . Images of spectacular scenes filled Lilith's mind , vistas of beauty , people wielding magicks , mythical beings walking down streets . Her eyes closed as she fell fast asleep , a delicate smile painted on her face .
The cloaked woman got off the bed and replaced her clothing , rolled Lilith over and patted her on the ass .
" Enjoy your bliss . "
She scanned the room , locating Lilith's purse , picked it up and pulled out a cell phone . Her fingers moved across the small keyboard then hit send and laid the phone on Lilith's ass .
" One more , then the hard part . "

Chapter 39

Jade was busy going over the copy for the Sunday morning edition . She took off her glasses , grabbed her cup of coffee and took a sip .

" Ah , that's better . Look at this junk . "

She flipped through a pile of papers , shaking her head in disgust .

" Welcome to Wicker county Jade . This place is so boring . If I wasn't so ethical , I would make up some news to spice up the paper . "

Movement outside her office window caught her eye . A woman with red hair quickly made her way past Jades narrow view .

" Patricia ? "

She got up and ran out the door . There was no one on the floor . She rubbed her eyes .

" Am I starting to see things ? Maybe I need to get some sleep . "

A large folded card sitting on a desk caught her attention . Her name was written on the outside . She picked it up and opened it .

" *Follow the white rabbit to safety , love Pandora* "

A shiver ran down Jade's spine . This was impossible . Her sister was in another state in a secure mental institution .

The front door flew open causing Jade's heart to skip a beat .

" Veronica ! You scared the hell out of me . "

" Sorry Jade . You need to come with me , your life is in danger . "

" What the hell are you talking about ? "

" Do you have a sister ? "

" Why would you ask me that ? Yes . I don't want to talk about her though . How did you know that ? "

" A man told me . "

" What man ? "

" His name is Donovan and I think he is hunting her down .

He inquired about you . This man is an assassin and he intends to kill her and probably you as well . We have to go now . "

Jade's eyes opened wide as she realized what Veronica was wearing , a black t-shirt with a big white rabbit on the front , the words " Down the hole we go again " written beneath .

" Follow the white rabbit . "

" What ? " Veronica looked at her shirt . " Oh , right . It is Lily's . "

" Let's go then . "

The two of them exited the building and made their way to Lily's convertible .

" Lily , Brad this is my boss Jade Hawthorne . We need to keep her safe from Donovan . "

" Understood . Everyone in the car . Brad you drive babe . "

Brad and the girls got in the car . He started it up .

" Where to Lily ? "

" The park of course . "

The convertible sped down the road heading to it's favorite parking spot by the pond .

" What about tomorrows paper . I didn't finish putting it together . "

Veronica held up the file .

" Considering what I have already seen this evening in addition to what is in here , that is the least of our concerns . By this time tomorrow , our lives will be very different I am afraid . "

Lily leaned over her seat to make eye contact with Veronica .

" What are you talking about chick ? "

" Project Awakening , my parents secret little project . They were attempting to awaken the hidden self in people , to find out what we are all truly capable of doing . "

" Sounds cool . What is the issue ? "

" They succeeded . They awakened something in my brother , some form of power . The projects head , Miranda Star , used combinations of substances and hypnosis to trigger something in him . After her success with my brother , she used her techniques on her two children Vander and Domino Star . "

" Wait . Domino ? That is the girls name that called me and told me you were in danger . How could she have know ? "

" Not sure . I haven't even gotten to the weird part yet . "

" Oh , well continue then . "

" She was murdered shortly after by Donovan . The kids were relinquished to Eric Kaid's custody . Thing is , he does not exist . He is not real . "

" How is that ? I have met him a couple times . He seemed real enough to me . "

" I am not clear on the details , but he is some kind of projection created to watch over those kids . He is like a puppet being controlled from a distance by his creator . "

" Do you know who ? "

" Ya . The last person I would ever have suspected to be involved in anything serious . "

" Who ? "

Chapter 40

Sabrina tossed and turned in her bed , her eyes moving under her eye lids . She had vivid dreams before but nothing like this . She awoke to the sound of scratching on her glass patio door . She opened her eyes , sat up and looked to see what woke her .

A blue gray cat sat peering into her bedroom . A butterfly covered bandana was wrapped around his neck .

" The dream . "

She jumped out of bed and tried in vain to open the door but her brother Andy always locked her in from the outside when he left so she couldn't leave the house and get into trouble .

" Dammit Andy ! I hate you ! " She kicked the glass hurting her foot .

She sat on her bed and massaged the painful area . She was sick of it . Every since their parents died Andy has taken care of her . His way .

He monitored her every activity , even having her teachers call him from time to time to let him know what she was in to . He was domineering and a slave driver . She cooked and cleaned to avoid his wrath and was never allowed any guest . School was the closest thing she had to a retreat but even there most of the kids avoided her in fear of Andy's response .

" Well Mr . Cat , I can't let you in or come out to you . You were in my dream and now you are here . I guess that means the dream will become real . If that's so , I just have to be patient and I will be free of this place and this life for ever . "

She removed all off her clothes and laid back down . Thoughts of freedom and pleasure swam in her mind causing a smile to form on her face .

" Just be patient . I will finally be free of my hell . "

Chapter 41

The sheriffs silver patrol cruiser pulled in behind a long blue sedan , headlights on and hazard lights blinking . Bakers woods hugged the outside of the curve were Victor was standing . He was looking down at something , lost in thought .

Mathew and grace exited the car and walked to him . A little off the road , leaning up against a tree , was Stacey's corpse , the words to Pandora written in blood on her exposed stomach . Grace retracted and covered her mouth .

" Grace calm the fuck down . You need to be sharp right now . Go call the coroner and have him retrieve her . " Mathew grabbed a smoke from his pocket and lit up .

Grace ran to the car and got on the radio . Her voice shaking as she dispatched the coroner . In the four years she had been a deputy , this was the first murder she ever encountered and she was not prepared for it .

" Victor , want to tell me what is going on ? "

" I made a horrible mistake Mathew . I am a god fearing man , have been my entire life . After the last few hours though , I feel my beliefs have been seriously flawed . I let that man into my house thinking he was an agent of the divine but he is nothing more than a murderer . "

" Are you referring to Donovan ? "

" Yes . Sheriff , he is a monster . He means to hunt those children down and kill them all . "

Mathews cellphone beeped .

" One moment Victor . "

It was another text from Mathew's taunter .

" *You think you are clever but I know better . My journey is near it's end . I want you to ponder the meaning of pain as I set your nerves on edge . I left you another present , come collect it when you can .* "

" Dammit ! I can't deal with this right now . "

" Mathew ? "

" Some one playing games with me as she has her way

with unwilling girls , this night has to come to an end before I do . "

" Yes . I feel the same . We are in to deep now Mathew . I don't see this ending well . Donovan is very dangerous . He is not to be taken lightly . "

" I got that feeling when I met him earlier this evening . " He looked toward his car and yelled . " Grace ! Get Andy to check out the Stevenson's , there has been another rape . "

Victor knelt down and closed Stacey's eyes . " I am so sorry child . If I had only known . Please forgive me . "

" Victor , you need to tell me everything you know . Leave your car here and ride to the station with us . I'll bring you back later to retrieve your car . "

" Yes . Yes , of course . "

He buttoned Stacey's shirt back up and laid his hand on her head . Tears ran down his face . " I truly am sorry . "

" Lets go Victor . "

Victor got up and made his way to the patrol cruiser . Grace open front passenger door for him and climbed in the back . Mathew started the car , pulled out and did a u-turn , heading back to the sheriffs department .

" Everything you know Victor . "

" Right . He is from the highest order of the church . From what I gathered he has been tracking this Pandora for over a year now . I think the children were unexpected , but he is determined to kill them saying they have been tainted by her . He is a mad man . I could see it in his eyes the last we spoke . "

" Don't worry . I will find him and bring him in . He won't hurt anyone else . "

" No . You don't understand . I told you he is very dangerous . He possess true power , the kind we have no defense against . You gun is hardly any match for him . He will kill you Mathew . "

" You mean like Reginald with his control over fire ? "

" I don't know exactly what he is capable of just that he is out of your league . I am at a loss figuring out how to deal with this . "

" We have to do something Victor . I won't have a madman running around my county killing children , super powered or not . If my gun don't work on him then I'll grab a bat , if that don't work a rock , what ever it takes we will stop him and get to the bottom of this Pandora mess . "

" I like your tenacity . I hope there is a way to end this horror show . Either way though , there is no turning back for me . I have lost all that I was and all that was mine . "

" How so ? " Grace interjected .

Victor turned his head to meet her gaze and sighed .

" Margret is enamored with Donovan and his ways . I tried to reason with her , explain to her what he is . She called me a traitor . Said I had been tainted and demanded I leave the house . She is gone to me , a different creature than she was yesterday . She has seen true power and now has a lust for it . "

" What an insane night . Mathew , why is all this happening to our corner of the world ? I am getting scared . What are we going to do ?"

" I don't know yet Grace . We just have to move a step at a time and keep our wits about us . "

Chapter 42

Nick was sitting on a moss covered stump . His jeans and shirt were filthy from trekking through the woods . He had been walking for hours , sometimes running when heard a loud noise . His hair was laced in strands of spider web , leaf bits stuck to them . He rubbed his left leg . It was still sore from the tumble he took earlier .

A figure emerged from the trees . Nick's heart jumped through his chest . He froze , not knowing what to do . As it came into the moonlight , he relaxed and stood up .

" You scared the hell out of me Eric or who ever . "

" You are starting to figure out your way . Good . "

" You don't have an aura . You are not real . Who is the real you ? "

" Some one who loves you . "

" I see . Will I ever meet the real you ? "

" That is guaranteed . I still care about all of you , even though , well you know . "

Nick sighed and nodded . He was confused by the thing that stood before him . Every since Pandora touched him , his night has gotten stranger and stranger . Who was Eric and why was he taking care of him and his mates ? Better question , what is he ?

" What is with the apple ? "

Eric was holding a green apple with a bite taken out of it . He tossed it up a caught it , then looked Nick in the eyes .

" I don't have any time left . You have to run to Hill park as fast as you can . " He pointed toward a clearing . " There is a dirt road not far . It goes straight there . Now Run . "

A white column of smoke descended from the sky . Nick ran for the clearing , knowing he would never see Eric again . Donovan and Tempest appeared before Eric . A smile crossed Donovan's face .

" Eric Kaid , you saved me the trouble of hunting you down . I do appreciate accommodating prey . "

Eric smiled as Donovan severed his head . His body falling

in an instant , blood spewing from his neck on the way down . His head fell at Donovan's feet . Donovan sheathed his blade , blood still dripping from it and turned to Tempest .

" Read him . Then find me . " Donovan sprinted into the clearing and ran after Nick . He quickly vanished from Tempest sight . Leaving her to do his grunt work .

She despised him , along with those they served . But her path was locked away when they wrapped her in her chains . A traumatic experience for an eight year old girl . That was twelve years ago . Since then she had been passed master to master as they needed her ways . Each of them cruel and hollow , capable of great atrocities . If only she had the strength to wrest that dagger away from Donovan . But such thinking would only earn his wrath .

Tempest sighed and lowered her hood . She rubbed her temples with her fingers and closed her eyes . Using even a small amount of her way while wrapped in bindings caused her great discomfort .

" The bastard could have loosen them a little . Screw it . "

She walked to the body and knelt down . As she went to touch it , the head spoke , causing her to jump to her feet and back away .

" Relax . I just have a message for you . "

He released the apple in his hand . It rolled toward her a bit then came to a rest .

" Pick it up and read it . "

Eric's body and head , along with all the blood around them , vanished before Tempest eyes . She walked to the apple and picked it up . Then turned it over and over in her hand . She took a deep breath and focused . A sharp pain formed from the rune on the back of her neck . She tensed up , tears running down her face . She worked through her misery and achieved clarity . A fuzzy scene began to form in her mind .

It was Hill park . The surface of the pond was dancing as rain drops struck it . Eight orbs of light hovered near the shore , each a different color . Next to them stood a man in rags . He had his back to her , tossing a green apple in the air and catching it over and over . He turned and looked into Tempest eyes and smiled . He continued throwing the apple into the air as he walked closer to her perspective until he appeared right before her .

" Hello Tempest . I am glad that prick is predictable to a fault . "

His eyes came to life , turning into a dance of lines oscillating colors on a sea of black . He took a bite of the apple , then wiped his mouth on his sleeve .

" How rude of me . I haven't introduced my self . I'm Agamemnon , Agamemnon Sin . "

Tempest shivered . Stories of house Sin floated on whispers from superiors when they thought her out of ear shot . Stories of their exodus at the hands of the veils architects . All but one .

" I understand the misery brought by these . " He rolled up a sleeve . Tight blue ropes of glyphs ran from his wrist to beneath his sleeve .

" The aggravation of having your ways restricted , nearly totally cut off from your core . Sealed tight . Only undone by a key for ever out of your reach . Or is it ? You lied to Donovan about young Reginald and for that I am grateful . It is apparent that you wish to be free of him and those he serves . "

He rolled his sleeve back up and turned his back to her view , apple still going up and down .

" Your ticket to freedom will soon present itself to you . It will only come once . Decline it and you are doomed to servitude until your demise . Tell your master the action is in the towns square . I look forward to meeting you . "

The orbs came together and formed Eric .

" Ah , hello love . Are you ready to end that conjuration . A decade is an impressive feat considering you are currently limited ? " Agamemnon reached the apple out to Eric .

" Absolutely . It has put a great strain on me . I have done everything I could to prepare our shining stars for what lies ahead , so let's get this over with . "

Eric took the apple and polished it on his shirt ,then turned his gaze to Tempest .

" I do hope you will join us . "

The vision ended .Tempest was on her knees . Her hair glistened from layers of sweat . She pushed her self up and brushed her self off .

" Could he really remove my bindings ? Could I really be free ? Shake it of girl . Just thinking like that will get you killed . "

She headed toward the clearing in search of her master , wondering what she would tell him and what lied in store for them in the towns square . She felt a sense of hope for the first time in her life .

Chapter 43

The Twilight Cinaplex was the only theater in Wicker county . Six screens of mind numbing entertainment .
" Ya ! *Zombies Run the Country* , I have been dying to see it . "
Curtis stepped up to the ticket window .
" One for the Zombies , please . "
" That will be eight dollars and twenty-five cents . "
He reached into his pocket and pulled out eight ones .
" I only have eight bucks , can I slide on the quarter ? "
" Sorry . I am not paying it . "
Curtis hung his head . What was he going to do with the rest of his Saturday night ?
" Hey mister , I have a quarter . "
Curtis turned to see Violet , a quarter resting in her open hand . He was awe struck . He had never seen such a beautiful creature . She had the look of a devious angel and smelled like ambrosia .
" Um , thanks . "
Vander grabbed his hand and examined it .
" What is with the piece of plaid around your finger , friend ? "
" Oh this . A strange girl gave it to me for giving her a ride . "
" Domino !? "
" Ya . How did you know that ? Is she a friend of yours ? "
" With out a doubt . Where is she ? Is she alright ? "
" Slow down dude . I dropped her off awhile ago . She was fine when I last saw her but I did get the sense she was in some kind of trouble . Now that I think of it , aren't the two of you a little young to be running about this late ? "
" Do you know where she went by chance ? "
" She said was that she was heading to where the moon never sets . Like I said , strange girl . "
Vander looked at Violet and smiled .
" I know where she is going . I hate to be a bother , but

could you give us a ride ? It is very important . "

Curtis shrugged his shoulders and glanced at the marque .

" I didn't want to watch a movie by my self anyways .
Come on let's get you reunited with your friend . "

" Thanks a million . " Violet hugged Curtis . " It is nice to
know we are not totally alone in this . "

" This ? "

Violet stepped back , put her hands behind her back and
smiled . " You will see . I have a feeling you already stepped
in it . "

Her statement made Curtis a little nervous . He headed to
his car waving his new friends to follow him . " Let's ride . "

Chapter 44

Nick sprung through a line of trees onto the dirt road . Dust flew into the air as he hit it side ways , spun and sprinted forward in a single move . He could here the sound of Donovan ripping through the tall grass in the clearing behind him .

" Damn it he's too fast . Did Eric even slow him down ? "

Nick put all he had into increasing his speed , but the futility of it quickly donned on him as his breathing became strained . He heard Donovan's feet hit dirt and panic took control . He put the last of his energy into a desperate sprint and rounded a bend in the road . An old wooden bridge lied a few feet ahead of him . It spanned a deep gorge where Balor creek had eaten away the dirt and rock over the centuries .

" You can't escape your fate boy . Stand still and I'll make it quick . "

Donovan's voice sounded chilling , yet in only angered Nick . He flew across the bridge making it to the other side as Donovan reached it .

The air suddenly became very cold . The sound of a thousand banshees coming from behind him caused Nick to loose his balance and fall down . He looked toward the bridge in time to see a formless ethereal mass surround the it . The wood near instantly rotted away causing it to collapse into the ravine , Donovan falling along with it .

Nick got to his feet and started walking toward Hill park . A faint smile crossed his face .

" Thanks Stacey . "

Tempest casually walked up to the ravine's edge . She glanced across the gap . Nick was nearly out of site . An ethereal female form walked next to him , holding his hand . She smiled , delighted at the irony of her master's prey getting away with the aid of some one he had already murdered .

The sounds of rocks tumbling accompanied by a low

annoyed growl
came from below her . A hand reached up and grabbed her
leg . She froze as Donovan used her to pull him self out .

" What kind of way does that boy posses master . There is
nothing left of the bridge ? "

Donovan's cloak was shredded . He was soaking wet and
covered in mud and vegetation . He ripped of the cloak ,
threw it into the ravine and took a deep breath .

" I am not sure it was him that destroyed it . I felt a
different kind of presence . It sucked the warm from the air .
Did you see any thing ? "

" No master . I just arrived . "

He pulled the coin from his pocket . It sat in the palm of
his hand , cold and idle . Donovan looked into the sky and
screamed , then his gaze snapped to Tempest .

" Why can't the coin find him ? He could not have gotten
very far . "

" I don't know master . "

He grabbed her arm and jerked her to him then on to her
knees . Pain shot through her legs and back on impact and
she let out a brief scream .

" What use are you ! "

Tempest started crying while struggling to get to her feet .
A mix of pain and anger contorted her face .

" You bastard ! I do everything you ask me to ,even when it
causes me pain and you have to take your anger out on
me . Do you know how strong you are ? You almost
snapped me in two . "

He glared at her while contemplating her value versus the
satisfaction of killing her . Considering the difficulties he has
had hunting these children , he needed all the help he
could get .

" I may have been to harsh . It has been an annoying night
and I have reached my breaking point . It will take cutting
all of their throats and plunging my dagger into Pandora to
calm me down . "

He pulled Tempest up straight and began to brush her off .
She retreated from him a couple of steps and wiped the

tears of her face .

" Fine . What did you learn from our fallen idiot ? "

Tempest glared at him silently , her breathing uneven , left eye twitching . She was done . It was better to be dead than treated this way . His dagger dangled from his lowered left hand . She turned her eyes to it and stepped forward , ready to leap for it when she got close enough . Her mind flashed to the message from Agamemnon . She hesitated at the possibility of a real way out , a way to freedom . She had to find out . She took a deep breath .

" He was in Hill park talking to a man in rags , something concerning the conclusion of their plan . "

" Plan ? Kaid and a bum ? "

" Yes master . I only caught the end of their conversation . "

" I thought you could go back as far as you desired . "

" Normally . Yes . When you release the glyph on my neck . I can barely function with these bindings so tight . "

" I see . Did I neglect to do that . Huh . " He shrugged as a malicious smile crossed his face . " Well ? What did you hear then ? "

" Town square . What ever they were talking about will happen in the town square and soon . "

Donovan reached his hand out to Tempest .

" I will try to be more considerate in the future . Let's go . "

She took his hand and closed her eyes , zipping around in a pillar of smoke made her queasy . He grasped the coin tightly in his hand and the two of them were enveloped in a column of white smoke . It flew off , quickly making it's way to the town square .

Chapter 45

" Why do you want me to grow up ? I am only six . Don't you like me anymore Domino ? "

Domino and Alexis walked down the side walk holding hands , Pink cradled in Alexis free arm . It was an upscale neighborhood , lavish houses with exotic cars in their driveways .

" I love you . I love all of you . That is why you need to grow up , so you can help protect them . "

Alexis had no response . It didn't make sense to her . She was only six years old . How could she ever protect the people she loved . Did Domino know something she didn't ? Was she truly powerful and too young to understand ? She was tired , shaken and hungry . She wanted to be home with Eric and her friends , serving tea to Pink . Life was good then . It was simple .

They came to the end of the subdivision . Houses turned to small offices and specialty shops . Domino pulled Alexis behind a florist shop and gave her the candy bar in her pocket .

" Stay right her and eat this . Don't make a sound . I will be back in a few minutes . Understood ? "

Fear shot through Alexis mind at the thought of Domino leaving her alone . Her lips puckered as she started trembling .

" No ! Don't leave me Domino . " She wrapped her arms around Domino's waster , dropping Pink in the process . " I'll be good . "

Domino pried Alexis from her and stroked the side of her face .

" I know you will . I need to take care of something . Just sit and eat that quietly and when I get back we will go find Vander and Violet and you can get some rest . " Domino closed her eyes and tried lessen the pain in her head . The strain only made it worse . A stream of tears ran down her face as she forced a smile .

Alexis complied . The thought of seeing Vander and Violet again calmed her down . She watched Domino go around the corner as she unwrapped her dinner .

Domino casually made her way down the street , staring into the night sky as she moved forward . She was tired herself but knew it would be some time before she got any sleep . It seemed the weight of the world rested upon her shoulders and it was not far from being the truth . Hard decisions awaited her , the lives of her loved ones laid in her hands as did the fate of many others . She knew it was futile to run from what she had to do . Her only desire now was to see this though while keeping what she treasured safe .

A set of headlights came from behind her . She picked her pace up slightly and looked forward . The car stopped not far from her . Deputy Andy exited the car and began to pursue her .

" Stop ! I said stop young lady ! "

She sprinted down the street . Andy took off after her . He was quickly gaining on her , his stride much larger than hers . As she passed the bakery , she came to a stop . She heard the sound of an air gun going off twice then a thud behind her . She turned around to see the cloaked woman holding a gun and Andy laying at her feet out cold . Domino bent down and removed Andy's keyring , tossing it to the feet of her savior .

" Good luck . "

The woman picked up the keys , threw down the gun and smiled at Domino .

" You as well . "

Domino turned and ran back to the florist . Alexis had her eyes closed , fingers covered in chocolate and Pink on her lap . The pavement and back wall of the florist shop had become her bed .

" Wake up Alexis . " Domino shook her . " Time to go . "

Alexis opened her eyes and rubbed them leaving a ring of chocolate around her right eye . She grabbed Pink and stood up still half asleep .

" You look a mess and so does your bear now . "

Alexis eyes opened wide and looked at Pink's arm where her sticky hand now gripped .

" Oh , I am so sorry Pink . "

" Don't worry I will wash the two of you up when we get to Vander and Violet . Let's move . "

Alexis reached out to take Domino's hand but Domino pulled away .

" Your not holding my hand with that sticky thing . One more move to make before we take a break."

She pulled out the cell phone and dialed .

" Hi my name is Domino . Listen Carefully . A good friend of your is in grave danger . Get to the Hawthorne newspaper and make it quick . "

Chapter 46

Stacey and Nick made it to Hill park . Donovan was nowhere to be seen . They were safe for the moment and Nick decided he needed to rest a minute .

" Are you ok Nick ? "

He ran his hand down her ice cold arm sending shivers through out his being . She pulled away from him and lowered her head .

" I am dead . You don't want to touch me . I am not even real anymore . I can't stand it . "

" Don't say that . You saved my life . You are as real as I am . "

" But look at me . You can see right through me and I know I am cold to the touch . How can I ever ... ? What is that ? " She pointed at the wand tucked in his belt .

" I am not really sure . "

She grabbed the tip of it . The heart began to glow . She smiled at looked at Nick with eager eyes .

" Nick . " her voice was aroused .

She licked her lips and pinned him to a tree . Her hands went to his face and her lips to his mouth . He could feel her . She was cold but the sensations she was giving him were very pleasant . He embraced her in return and the two of them slid down to the ground .

As she kissed him , she grew warmer and more solid . With in moments a full blooded Stacey was having her way with him . She had come to life from his touch , warm and naked . She was overwhelmed with joy and bliss . Nick was not far from it .

" Well , well . Someone is having fun . "

Nick and Stacey paused and looked up . Lily was hovering over them , a huge smile on her face .

" Wow , a couple of adorables playing in my park and I didn't get an invite . Shame on you . I am tired of missing out . "

Nick pulled his t-shirt back on and stood up . Stacey

blinked and she was clothed in ethereal garments .

" How did you do that ? I would love to learn that trick . "

" I am a ghost . It comes with the package . "

" A ghost ? " Veronica walked up behind Lily . " You are Stacey and Nick right ? So he got you then ? "

" Ya . He slit my throat , but I apparently am harder to get rid of than that . What do you know about all this . "

Veronica explained what she had learned to the two of them . How she figured it all started and the fact Eric was not real . That he was some form of construct controlled by an old friend of hers , Persephone .

They listened intently and let it all soak in .

" I would like to meet this Persephone . Not fair her knowing us so well be we no nothing of her . " Stacey was resolved to continue on with life even though she was dead . Nick woke her up and she was ready to figure things out .

" I am sure you will . For now , we need to find a way to keep safe . "

" I have that covered . " Lily reached her hand out to Brad . " Red phone babe . "

He reached into his pants , pulled out a red cell phone and handed it to her . She flipped it open and hit call . There was only one number programmed into the red phone .

" Yo , little Penny , mandatory end of the world party at the park . Spread the word . "

Chapter 47

Persephone felt renewed . For nine years she carried the burden of running the conjuration known as Eric . She had no regrets though . Nine wonderful children had enriched her life and reminded her that joy was always possible when you are ready to embrace it and return it in full to those who are important to you .

" What a spectacular night . Watching all this unfold is a dream I had almost given up on . How about you ? Are you nervous ? "

Zia closed her book and climbed out of the recliner . She stretched to the sky and smiled .

" Me , Nervous ? Not even . I am eager to to this . It is time I came out of my cocoon . "

" Well , I am glad to here that . So are you finished studying ? Can you pull this off now ? "

" Ya . Now we just have to wait . I still do not understand how I know this stuff , but I guess that is a mystery I will figure out later . " Zia made her way to the wooden box . She opened its lid and pulled out a black silk cloak which she threw on over her butterfly pajamas . " So how does this look on me? " She turned to face Persephone .

" Cute and dangerous , it suits you . "

Zia smiled as she twirled around . Her cloak flowed around her like a silent dance partner . A swarm of ethereal butterflies formed around her and began to flutter about , occasionally landing on her for a quick kiss . She delighted at the presence of her new found friends . They made her feel safe and powerful .

" There are a lot more of them than when you resurrected Felix . Your power is growing rapidly . I am very impressed . " Persephone pondered on how quickly her shining stars and Zia embraced their ways . It took her a decade just to master the basics of Anima and these children had already reached beyond the foundations of their ways in a single night . She was very pleased . Her dream of bringing down the veil was now in sight .

Zia quit twirling and made her way to a bay window , her entourage following her . She stared out at the specks of moon light reflect off the falling rain drops . Her mind drifted to thoughts of Casidy , her treasure . Zia wished she could have told Casidy everything , but her mother swore her to secrecy . Her mood turned dark . She could not stand to see her sister in turmoil . If only she could have told Casidy the truth then her love would not have to suffer . She turned back toward Persephone .

" I hope all this is worth it . Do not get me wrong . I love my new abilities and it is all very exciting , but what Casidy had to go through makes me queasy . I will not be happy with any of this until I know she is happy as well . "

" I get that . I know who she is to you . I know how hard it was for you to keep quiet . But I promise love , everything will be as it should and I know Casidy will forgive you . She will understand . "

" I hope you are right . "

Zia shifted her focus to the butterflies . They stopped flying about and hovered in place . They began whispering in unison . The words were so soft she could barely hear them . She licked her lips to moisten them then smiled .

" It is time to go Persephone . It is time to get this night over with . "

Persephone grabbed her car keys and headed to the door . Zia fell in behind her .

" Are you going to take that book ? "

" I memorized what I need for tonight . "

" We aren't coming back here again sweety . Grab the book . "

" Oh . I was not aware . "

Zia grabbed the book and headed out the door after her friend . The butterflies followed their mistress to the car serene and happy with the life she has given them and the path they will take her down .

Chapter 48

The Moonscape was once packed on a Saturday night . From bumper cars to pool tables , it had everything to entertain the masses . That was until it was shut down due to safety violations and for the last three years it has sat here , empty of life and run down .

" Well this is it . Eric used to bring Domino and I here when we were little . We had a lot of fun , I remember . " Vander looked around , soaking up the memories he made in this place .

" It's all fallen apart . Why would she have us meet here . " Violet was not impressed . She wanted a soft bed and some one in it to warm her up . This place simply was not up to par .

" She knew I would remember . It is not that bad in here . We will just chill until she shows . "

Curtis flipped a light switch . A row of lights over the concession stand came on . " Hey , power works . "

" Neat . Check the water . "

Curtis went behind the counter and turned on the faucet . It sputtered for a moment then fresh water poured out . " Yep it is on as well . Do you think they knew you were coming ? "

" They ? "

" I don't know . This whole thing is way to whack for me . "

Domino and Alexis walked in . Vander's eyes lit up as he ran and snatched Alexis of her feet . He kissed her all over and squeezed the stuffing out of her .

" Hey little bit ! I am so glad to see you are ok . "

She wrapped her arms around his neck and kissed him on the cheek .

" Thanks Vander . I missed you too . "

Domino pulled her off him .

" Go wash up then it is to bed with you . " She pointed at a sink . " Go on ! "

" Hey chill Domino . I wasn't finished giving her lovin . "

" Sorry . It had been a long night . She needs to get to sleep . Make her a bed over there by the bumper cars . "

" Make her a bed ? "

" If you can make a gambling room , a bed should be no problem . "

He shook his head and walked to the bumper cars . A flash of colored lines turned a car into a nice soft bed .

Alexis finished washing the chocolate off her and Pink then ran and jumped into the bed .

" I like it . It is super cushy . Thanks Vander . "

" No problem cuteness . Now get some sleep . "

She closed her eyes and was out in seconds .

" Well , I will leave you all to yourselves . I am going home and crash myself . " Curtis made his way toward the door .

" Hold it . " Domino grabbed his arm . " take this and give it to ghost girl . " She handed him a folded letter .

" Ghost girl ? "

" You will know what I am talking about . Oh , enjoy the party . "

" Party ? " Curtis cell phone went off . He flipped in open . " Hello ? "

" *Yo babe , it's little penny* "

Curtis turned to Domino . " How do you do that ? " He shrugged his shoulders as he left the building .

" Well oh great leader , what do we do now ? " Violet's was being sarcastic .

Domino stared at Alexis as she slept . She wiped a tear from her face before anyone could see it , then turned to answer Violet's question .

" Vander is going to make us a big bed then the three of us are going to make love to one another . "

Chapter 49

Jules was standing in the town square , another bland and boring sight . She could here faint voices coming from the other side of the courthouse . A man wearing rags was sitting in the street drinking something wrapped in a brown paper bag . A small man ran toward her waving his arms in the air .

" This is bad , so bad . Mistress will be very upset . Yes she will . You ! How are you here ? " He pointed at Jules as he got closer . " Skid can not do anything about Pandora but he can deal with you . "

His arms turned into sharp blades . He waved them wildly as he ran at her only to be tripped by the man in rags . He jumped up ready to slice who ever made him fall but froze at the sight of Agamemnon .

" Sin ! No not Sin ! Help ! Help ! " He ran as fast as his little legs would take him and disappeared around the corner .

" He doesn't seem to like me . Oh well , I'm sure he ran to tell his mistress what he saw . Works for me . " Agamemnon smiled .

" Sorry . Who are you and what was that ? "

" Me ? Just a friend . That little rodent was a skit . They run about on this side of things reporting any thing not right to their mistress . No worries , after seeing me he probably forgot about you . I wonder what got him riled up . " He glanced at the courthouse . " Maybe you should take a look . I'll bet there is something of interest to you . "

" Um ok . Thanks for the help , I think . "

" Sure anytime . Have fun . "

Chapter 50

Donovan scanned the barely lit square , gripping the hilt of his blade in anticipation of a fight . He was at the end of his patience and would not tolerate any more obstacles . He growled .

" Well , were is the action you spoke of ? "

" I can only tell you what I saw . I am not a mind reader nor can I read the future . They said the final stage of their plan would happen here and it would be tonight . "

" Something better come of this or I am going to reevaluate your worth to me . "

Tempest contemplated the meaning of his words . If she was of no value to him , he would surely kill her out of sheer amusement . If something did not happen soon , she would be screwed . Surely Agamemnon would not set her up only to die at Donovan's hands . That would serve him no purpose . She cleared her mind of worry .

" I am sure you will not be displeased . The affair sounded very important . Something will happen . "

" I hope you are right . I grow tired and look forward to some sleep . I wish to have happy dreams when I do rest , so we need to end these abominations and soon . "

" Yes . Of course . I look forward to this ending as well . Perhaps you will loosen my bindings a little and allow me some comfort . "

He stared at her with a look of amusement . She has grown bold since they arrived in Wicker county . Her mouth nearly costing her life a couple of times , only saved by Donovan's need for her talents .

" You think so ? It simply will never happen . Those bindings are to keep you in check . You are dangerous and untrustworthy . They knew that when you were but a child hence the bindings . To loosen them would be a horrible mistake . The monster in you would surface , then I would have to kill you . We don't want that , do we ? "

Tempest knew it was futile to ask such things . She has

spent her entire life wrapped in the bindings placed on her by her own father . They were just loose enough for her to taste a little of the power she possessed but not enough for her to breath . She needed to keep Donovan off balance , at least until her way out reveals itself .

" No . I don't want to die , especially at your hands . "

" I thought not . Now no more about your wants or comforts . You are a tool , no more and you need to accept that . "

" Yes master . "

Mathew turned onto Main Street and made his way toward the sheriffs department . Victor pointed out the front window .

" It's him . Why is he here ? Does he know I betrayed him ? I have a feeling this is my last night alive Mathew . "

" Don't say that . I won't let him touch you . I give you my word . Grace draw your gun . Don't let him breath . "

" Yes sir . "

Grace removed her revolver from it's holster , spun the cylinder round in its seat and pulled back the hammer .

Mathew pulled onto the lot and parked next to Grace's patrol car . Grace exited first , training her gun on Donovan as she climbed out of the back seat . Mathew followed suit .

" Stay in the car Victor . I will leave the keys in the ignition . If all else fails , drive away and don't look back . "

" As you say . But I have a very bad feeling about this . "

Donovan glanced toward the new arrivals . He sighed at the sight of drawn weapons and slowly walked toward the patrol cars .

" Don't take another step Donovan ! " Mathew gripped his gun tight and got a steadier aim . " Get on the ground or I will shoot you . "

" Is that so ? " He looked to his side and glared at Tempest . " Is this part of the so called plan ? Are you trying to set me up Tempest ? "

" No . Never master . I am no fool . They stand no chance . " She looked at Mathew . " Please put the guns down before you anger him . I don't want to see any more unnecessary deaths . "

Mathew aimed the gun at her . His heart was racing , adrenaline flowed through his blood . His nerves had reached their limits . He did not care who these two were or what they were capable of . He was ready to end this nightmare .

" You are just as bad as he is . You defend him , knowing what he has done . You are equally a murderer . What kind of people hunt down and kill children ? "

Victor exited the car and walked up beside Mathew . He placed his hand on top of the gun , pushed it toward the ground then looked at Grace and motioned for her to do the same .

" This is not the way . Their has been to much violence this evening as it is . If they want me , so be it . My life is not worth sacrificing the two of your lives . "

Donovan's face broke into a smile . He contemplated the sheer stupidity of the mortals that stood before him .

" Are you serious ? Why would I worry about the likes of you ? You are a weak man Victor . Your faith has failed you . Go hide under a rock until this is over . I would not waste my blade on such a pitiful creature . At least Margret knows where her loyalties lie . "

" Yes . She does . God will deal with her and me as well . "

" God ? You are a fool . There is no god . Just blind idiots who kneel to an idea . I am an agent of the true rulers of the world . If you need to bow to a divine being , it is them you should kneel before . "

Mathew raised his gun and aimed it at Donovan . He fired four rounds , each of them hitting Donovan square in the chest . Shell casings falling to Victor's feet .

Tempest dove to the ground so she would make less of a target . Donovan was bullet proof . She was not and had no intentions of dying when she was so close to freedom .

Donovan never flinched . The bullets penetrated his clothing only to bounce of his skin . He put a finger in one of the holes in his shirt and begin to growl .

" Very stupid man . I had no quarrel with you until now . I

am going to make you eat that gun boy . "

He drew his dagger and lunged at Mathew . Grace got off one round but missed due to his speed . Victor closed his eyes knowing the end was now inevitable .

As Donovan got with in striking distance a black puff of smoke came between him and Mathew . A black gloved hand shot out , palm hitting Donovan in the chest , sending him flying across the street into one of the court houses columns . It shattered on impact , knocking Donovan out .

Pandora stepped from the smoke and grabbed Grace . She pulled her close , kissed her then tossed her in Mathews direction . She collided with Mathew , both falling to the ground . Grace starting taking off her clothes .

" I want you Mathew . Take me right here . "

He pushed her away and slapped her .

" Get a grip on your self deputy ! "

Donovan was starting to stir . His vision was still blurry and his head was spinning but he had no time to worry about such things . He pulled himself to his feet and staggered forward , dagger still clutched in his hands . He was very annoyed .

Pandora removed her right glove and shoved Victor to the ground via his face . He screamed . Flashes of horrible images raced through his mind . Forty plus years a hellfire sermons came back to haunt him .

Grace ran to her car , jumped in and sped out of the parking lot . Mathew ran to his car yelling.

" Grace stop ! I am sorry , please stop ! "

He was quickly loosing sight of her car as he jumped in his cruiser . He had really messed up . Not just slapping her . He had been messing up for awhile now , with Sam , the girls , Grace . He was lost and saw no end to the ride he had been on .

Donovan watched as the two cruisers sped from the scene , then turned his attention to the others .

Tempest was pushing her self up as Pandora reached her gloved hand out to her .

" Hurry . He is coming . " Pandora grabbed her by the arm

and pulled her to her feet .
  Donovan ran toward them , blade raised above his head .
  " No way are you escaping ! "
  Pandora pulled Tempest in close to her and flipped
Donovan off .
  " Bet me . "
  The puff of black smoke moved to cover them and in an
instant they were gone .
  Donovan fell to his knees , looked up and screamed . He
was shaking from the fury that flowed through him . He
gritted his teeth and got to his feet , walked to Victor and
picked him up by his neck .
  " Let's go traitor . "

Chapter 51

Jules walked to the other side of the court house . Two patrol cars were quickly leaving the scene . Donovan had Victor by the back of his neck . Jules ran at him , rage returned as thoughts of his death crossed her mind . A column of white smoke surrounded the two of them . It darted into the sky . Jules was determined not to loose him and willed herself to follow . The world bent before her and she went soaring through the sky , hot on the tail of the smoke . It landed at in the yard of the parsonage at St . Malachi's .

Jules hit some form of barrier and fell to the ground as Donovan and Victor entered the house . She got up and charged the barrier only to be knocked down again .

" For the love of all I hold dear . "

She got up and closed her eyes . She focused all her rage into her fist and punched the barrier before her . She felt it give a little and it became visible to her . A dark crack tainted its otherwise flawless surface . She growled , focused all her energy into her fist again and took another swing at it . A small areas of the barrier shattered , creating an opening large enough for her to slip through .

She made her way onto the parsonage lawn and walked through the wall in search of Donovan . He was standing in the living room , holding Victor by the back of his neck . Margret was facing him , a confused look on her face .

" I don't understand . What did she do to Victor ? "

" She touched him and he went mad . "

Victor was babbling to himself . Nonsense words and noises were all he could manage . He looked at Margret and began to cry . He tried to talk to her , but the language he spoke was his and his alone .

" That horrid woman . What has she done to you ? "

" I am sorry Margret . He is beyond hope . If you don't take action , his soul will be lost for ever . "

" What do I have to do ? "

He handed her a blade . " Kill him . "

She took the blade from Donovan .

" I am sorry Victor . We must follow the path god has laid before us . Mine is clear as is yours . "

She stabbed him in the chest . He screamed in agony , so she stabbed him again and again until he made no more noise . She was covered in his blood . A stream of it ran down her face and into her mouth , her first taste of blood and she liked it .

" You are truly a faithful woman Margret . I think you would be well suited to take Victor's place in the church . I will make the arrangements . We will need the congregation's support in the matter at hand . I will leave that to you . "

" Thank you master Donovan . I will not fail you . I will not fail god . "

" I truly believe that . "

" What of your assistant ? What will you do about her ? "

" I tried to bring her back . " He glanced at the dagger at his side . " But something is blocking me . I will find her and she will die for her treachery . This I promise . "

" Murderers . Nothing but murderers . " Jules was staring Donovan down . She screamed and the furnishings in the room each split into two halves as if they were cut by a very sharp sword .

Donovan grabbed his dagger . The runes on it began to glow . Jules head began to spin . She gasped for breath as her energy was being drained . Donovan moved in on her .

" You are mine now . "

A massive puff of purple smoke surrounded Jules . The smell stopped Donovan in his tracks .

" Vixen ? "

With in seconds it vanished taking Jules with it .

Chapter 52

A vast emptiness . Daniel , Agamemnon and Ivan stood staring into the deep black nothingness before them . Their forms lit from some unseen source . The only sounds were of three breaths and three heartbeats .

" Where is this ? " Ivan was a bit nervous . He had gotten used to a barrage of sights , sounds and smells and now there was nothing .

" This is my void . " Agamemnon turned pointing at the four corners of his vast domain of nothing .

" How can you own nothing ? "

Daniel started laughing . " It is not nothing . It is open potential . A space to manipulate at your choosing . Somewhere no one may tread without his permission . "

" Potential ? "

Agamemnon waved his hand . The blackness lit up with thousands of colored lines , scrambling around each other like static on a television . Columns of green stone took form followed by a blue stone floor and with in a couple of minutes they were standing in a large luxurious room , blackness looming outside the columns . A king size bed covered in black and blue silks sat in the center . It frame was of polished blue metal , three stone carvings of naked women sat on top . A bar with several liquid filled glass containers sat next to it .

" Potential . " Agamemnon looked at Ivan . " In here I am not bound , my ways of void and pattern work flawlessly . Life , existence is all about potential . Potential creations , sensations , knowledge , bliss . This place is my canvas , my home and my prison . But that will soon change . "

" When you become unbound you mean ? "

" You are a very smart boy and your way will be of great value . I am very pleased you decided to join house Sin . "

The blackness shimmered and Pandora stepped into the void towing Tempest behind her .

" Look who decided to accept your offer love . "

A smile crossed Agamemnon's face as he made his way to them . He embraced Pandora and gave her a welcome home kiss .

" Welcome home love . Excellent performance out there . I wish I had seen the look on that bastards face when you embarrassed him . Your control has grown rapidly since we met . I am very pleased . "

Pandora stared into his eyes with a look of wonder . Until him , she could never touch someone with out dire consequences . He brought her into his life and loved her . Her way transforming from a curse to a powerful tool as her heart was filled with joy . She was home and ready to play after a hard nights work .

" You know how to make me feel wanted . I adore you for that . "

He released his hold and turned his attention to Tempest . He took her hand and pulled her to him , embraced her and pressed his lips to hers . She started to retreat , but the sensation was pleasant so she gave into it and returned the kiss .

" Welcome to your new home sweet Tempest . The key to those bindings will soon be in my grasp and all of us will break free and embrace our full selves . "

" What of Donovan ? That blade can cause me great agony even a a distance . "

" As long as you are here it has no effect and you will remain here until the key arrives . "

He let her go and walked to the bar . In a small drawer was a purple colored bud of plant matter . He crumbled a large portion onto a paper , rolled it up and blew on the end of the joint setting it aflame .

Daniel instructed Ivan to stay clear of the smoke then headed to it's source .

" Vixen . It had been awhile since I have smelled that aroma . "

Agamemnon took a drag and passed it to Daniel which handed it to Pandora after hitting it . She took a large drag , every muscle in her body relaxed . She giggled as she

exhaled and started to hand it back to Agamemnon .
Tempest intervened , taking it from her .

" I am in this far . I may as well go in all the way . " She
took a long drag and handed it to Agamemnon . The smoke
slowly pored from the corners of her mouth as she was
overcome by a serene feeling . " Wow . What else do you
have for me ? "

Pandora looked at Agamemnon , a question on her lips .

" Yes love as I have said before . If you make contact with
her in the void she will become immune to your touch . "

Pandora grabbed Tempest hand and pulled her to the
bed .

" Come play with me awhile , we have some down time . "

Tempest climbed onto the bed and took her cloak off ,
tossing it to the floor . Pandora quickly joined her and lied
down . She pulled Tempest onto her and began to show her
some of the pleasures that come with being part of house
Sin .

Chapter 53

White and black lights took turns illuminating the end of the world party . Dark techno beats sent a sea of flesh into a frenzy . A moment of lightly clothed dancers , grinding against one another , followed by a barrage of bright colors moving on a black canvas .

Four black vans housing massive speakers formed a tight square , each with a different color dragon painted on the hood . A platform stood in the center , twice as high as the vans . A man with black dreads stood upon it , surrounded by keyboards and video screens . He swayed with the beats he sent out . Sweat ran down his face , creating shimmers of light against his dark complexion .

A light rain began to fall on the energetic crowd . They threw their hands into the air a screamed a salute in unison to natures gift . The wind picked up , distributing fresh air and rain among them . There pace quickened as the elements cooled them off .

Brad stood in awe as he watched Lily and Veronica seduce each other to the beat that heightened their desires . Veronica's hands were locked behind her head . Her body twisting with the music as Lily's hands and lips explored her . Each new discovery broadening Veronica's smile and Lily's need to bed her .

" This is our back up ? We are entering no man's land and she throws a party . " Jade's voice was strained .

Brad bent over , grabbed his stomach and laughed .

" Take a chill pill girl . "

He pointed to a pair of girls dancing together .

" The short one with glasses is Dr . Melony Contrace , PhD in biochemistry and Lily's specialty supplier . The tall blond with her is Boom Boom . Guess why we call her that . "

He turned her attention to a middle aged man with three girls .

" That is papa K , Lily's dad , ex-marine , volunteer firefighter , all around adrenaline junkie . He carries an arsenal in his truck and he knows how to utilize it. The man on the platform is mix master Black Dragon. He can do incredible things with anything that takes juice. Everyone here plays hard, but they all know their ways better than most and when it comes to trouble, they will always have your back. "

" Well I stand corrected. I have seen troubling days before, the metropolitan riots, panic from black outs, protest over the execution of a famous serial killer. But this, this is all way out of my league and for the first time since I was a child, I am terrified at the ramifications. How can we possibly deal with super natural powers when yesterday we did not even believe in their existence, at least I didn't. "

Brad shrugged his shoulders and grabbed her hand. He pulled her into the fray of dancers and put his arms around her.

" You just go with the flow. Either we can handle it or we can't. Fussing about it won't solve anything. Will we live through this ? Who knows ? But if I am going to meet my end soon, I am going to enjoy my self now. "

Jade wondered what his intentions were, then realized the futility of worrying about it. She relaxed and moved in close. Her heart skipping a beat as he grabbed her ass and pulled her in tight.

" I guess you are right pretty boy. Let's have some fun. "

Curtis slowly made his way down the parks main drive. He could see the lights flickering off the windows of a couple dozen cars. He made a circle around them until he found a good spot for his baby to rest. He got out and patted her on the hood. He made his way toward the core of the action, scanning the beautiful women as he walked through the fray.

" Yo Curtis, come chat with me. "

Little Penny was waving him to her. A bright red pony tail laid on her shoulder, red and black t and shorts painted on her tight body. Her hips moved side to side with the music as she licked her lips. Curtis eagerly made his way to her side.

" He little girl , what do you know ? "

" A little of this and a lot of that . Welcome to one strange night . "

" Strange ? Girl my night can't get any stranger . If only I could show you what I have seen . "

" You mean like a dead girl walking . " She glanced over her shoulder then back . " Or dancing for that matter . "

" Ghost girl ? "

" Ya she's a ghost . A lively one at that . "

" Damn , how does that girl know what she knows . I am glad they are friendlies . "

" What girl ? "

" Domino . She knew I would be at this party and that ghost girl would be here . "

" Wow . Neat . "

" Where is she ? I need to give her a message . "

Penny pointed toward the pond . Nick and Stacey were dancing together . Their eyes staring only at each other . Their movements were slow and deliberate , Stacey flashing from real girl to frightening apparition as the light changed back and forth .

" Wild ain't it ? " Penny slapped Curtis on the back .

" Ya . It is . "

He grabbed her in a bear hug , picking her up off the ground , and planted a kiss on her forehead .

" I loves ya you adorable creature . "

He returned her feet to the ground and gave her another kiss for good measure .

" I am going over to say hi . Don't vanish on me now . I am no where done with you fine thing . "

" I hope not . I'll be around . Come grab me when you are ready for some fun . "

She licked her lips as she walked away from him in search of a diversion or two to bide her time .

Curtis made his way through the crowd toward the mesmerized lovers on the outskirts of the party . They were locked in a kiss , slowly moving in circles , gently holding one another . They were oblivious to the world around them

, lost in each others embrace , wanting nothing more than what they currently held .

As he approached he felt the temperature drop . The air was chilled around them , their breath a visible mist . Curtis shivered as he came to a stop .

" Excuse me , um ghost girl , I have a letter for you . "

He reached into his pocket , pulled out the note Domino had given him and reached it out to her . She let go of Nick and took the note .

" Who is this from , um I didn't catch your name . "

" Oh , I'm Curtis and the letter is from a young lady I keep running into , Domino . "

" Domino ! " Nicks voice was excited .

" Ya she is a strange one , cool but strange . "

Stacey opened the letter and read it . Her eyes got wide and a temporary flash of anger crossed her face . She folded it up and handed it to Nick .

" What does it say babe ? " Nick put it in his pocket .

" We have to go . Some one needs our help . " She patted Curtis on the arm , her touch was chilly but pleasant . " If Domino trust you then I do as well . Thank you for any help you have give her . "

" I guess the two of you need a ride . "

" No , but thank you . The letter says it is important we get to our destination on foot . " She took Nick's hand . " Let's go love . I have something to finish . Enjoy the party Curtis . I am sure we will all see each other again . "

" What just happened ? What was that smoke ? How did my furniture become all chopped up ? " Margret was both excited and upset . She had never witnessed any thing like it . The word " Power " flashed over and over in her mind .

" Vixen . Only one of the old ones would have access to it . It seems we are dealing with more than I anticipated . That girl . How could she posses the way of Thresholds ? These children are far stronger than they should be . I have dealt with people touched by that wicked woman before . They never possessed Anima or Threshold or anything serious for that matter . "

A ball of bright light shot into the house from above . It hovered in front of Donovan a moment then stretched into a thin line of intense light . Margret passed out from the presence it emitted , Donovan fell to his knees . The room became so bright he had to close his eyes from the pain . The line exploded into waves of light and a figure stepped from it . She radiated and immense presence . Her long white hair reached to below her ass , tied of every other inch with black ribbon . Her eyes were swirls of colors , screaming faces floating in and out of the chaos as she looked around the room .

" On your feet Donovan . "

He opened his eyes and stood .

" Mistress Eno . I was not expecting you . Forgive me my failings . "

" Which seem to be adding up this eve , don't they ? "

" Yes mistress . "

" Pandora still walks , you lost Tempest to the enemy and you have not managed to deal with even one of her new toys . "

" The girl Stacey and that fire wielder are both dead . I will finish the rest of them mistress . "

" I thought you were smarter than that Donovan . Reginald still lives . You were deceived . As to Stacey , you only made her stronger when you took her physical life . You got cocky and messed up . You should have bound her first . "

Donovan was beside himself . Until now , he had a flawless record . No prey ever escaped him . He was ashamed and feared his mistress wrath . She was one of the few people he was truly terrified of .

" Please forgive me . I am in over my head . "

" Yes , you are . I don't blame you , so relax . I am equally to blame for your lack of success . It only recently came to my attention as to who we are dealing with here . "

" Mam ? "

" Agamemnon Sin is behind the events this evening and where ever he is , my big sister is bound to be close . "

" House Sin . I don't understand . I thought they were bound and powerless . "

" You are an idiot . They don't need their ways to be a serious problem . They are centuries wise and more cunning than you could ever fathom . To underestimate them is sheer suicide . I am taking over here . "

Eno waved her hand . A woman appeared kneeling beside her . Her platinum hair was as long as her mistress but undone and wild . It nearly covered her glowing green eyes and near perfect face .

" My sweet Gyslia , it is time to play . "

" I am always eager mistress . "

" Good . I need Hill park secured . Find some one competent and set them to the task . "

Gyslia got up and put her hands behind her back . She leaned in toward Eno and smiled . " Any thing for you . "

Eno turned to Donovan and crossed her arms . " Wake that woman . I have a use for her . Then go do something useful . "

" Yes mistress . "

Chapter 55

Jules was engulfed in a swirling mass of purple smoke . Her anger soon calmed and was replaced with a serene feeling . Time seemed to lose meaning as she drifted about . Her mind became clearer and sharper . The smoke began to recede . When it had mostly dissipated , she was standing in the deep of Baker's forest . A multitude of dull colorless trees stood before her , but off to her right a gleam caught her eye . She turned to see three massive trees . They were flowing with color and radiating bright light . In the center was a woman , floating just above the ground , eyes closed and arms folded over her chest . She had long black hair that laid on the ground beneath her and was wearing a thin white gown , the color of her flesh bleeding through . A swarm of florescent butterflies of various colors flew over her in a surreal dance . To one side of her was a purple velvet couch with black wood trim holding two gentlemen . One was sitting . He was middle aged with black and gray hair cut short . He was wearing a black leather suit , a blue butterfly on his jacket . The other was laying down , his head on his partner's lap . He looked early twenties , black bushy hair and a goatee . He donned a black Victorian era outfit , a red butterfly on his sleeve . They where both puffing on a hooka . Each time blowing out various colors of smoke .

" Look what we have here John . " The elder looked down and smiled .

" Yes , yes my sweet Wayne , it's a wayward girl . You are on the wrong side of things aren't you ? " He pointed at Jules .

" I am ? I can't tell any more . Which side is real ? " She placed her finger to her mouth and shook her head .

" Why both my dear . " replied Wayne . " They are one split in two . Our side and your side . But you walked to our side and that is curious and I like curious . "

" Pretty much unheard of really . " John added .

" I think I understand . So what are you two doing here

and who is she " Jules pointed to the floating woman .

" Well , we are here to watch over her until the time comes for her to wake up . As to who she is , that is an old friend of ours , Samantha Rain . " Wayne took a long drag and smiled .

" The sheriffs wife ? I thought she died . "

" What is death ? Do you know little one ? " John sighed and shook his head .

" How am I supposed to know something like that ? "

" You can't . That is the beauty of it all . There will always be mysteries no matter how much you learn . That's what keeps a soul in constant growth . But you know what you know and you will learn more , a lot more . You just have to go with the flow of things . "

Jules scratched her head . " Um sure , I'll try to remember that . "

" How adorable . You confused the girl even further John . This is becoming amusing . "

" I do strive to please my love . " He kissed Wayne's hand .

Jules pondered the meaning of Johns words and tried to put them into perspective with the eight plus hours . She remembered the horror of seeing the person she cherished most murdered , the strange little hateful thing , the man in rags and his cryptic talk and the way she felt when she was standing before Donovan . Her eyes got wider and a small smile crossed her face .

" Look . I think the girl is starting to understand . " John smiled and kissed Wayne on the cheek .

" It does appear so my pet . Tell me girl what do you know now that you didn't know before you came here ? "

Jules smile grew bolder as she took a deep breath of the smoke that lingered before her . She exhaled and licked her lips . " Nothing . I know nothing . My mind is empty and ready to be filled with the truth . Everything thing I thought I knew is subject to scrutiny because it is mostly lies . I need to find the truth of things and maybe then I will truly be alive . "

" Wow . I was expecting a shrug from you to be truthful . "

Wayne leaned back and smiled . " It seems you are getting the picture . I think our friends are going to pull it off this time love . "

" Yes . The board is in their favor this time . I will be delighted the day the veil falls and if this girl is an indication of how serious they are , it won't be long . "

Jules walked closer to the couch and sat on the ground before them . " Who are you friends and what do they want with me ? "

" Ah well that's a delicate subject . " Wayne leaned forward and patted her on the head . " Those answers are not mine to tell . "

" You don't know ? "

" I did not say that . I am simply not going to tell you . It is not my place . "

" I understand . "

" Good , good you are a smart girl . "

The butterflies began to glow and became very excitable , diving down to Sam then back up for another dive . The wind began to blow and the trees swayed to its tune . The surrounding ground burst into a sea of color as thousands of wildflowers erupted from the dirt . A soft rain began to fall , each drop sparkling like a falling prism .

" Rain ? " John scratched his head . " I haven't see rain in centuries . "

" No . Not since the veil . This is going to be spectacular . I am glad we decided to be part of it . " Wayne laid his hand on Johns face and softly patted .

" Indeed . " John closed his eyes and relaxed , enjoying the rain as an old friend nearly forgotten .

Jules reached up with a cupped hand , catching rain drops until she held a puddle of water . She tipped her hand so it ran down her arm . It swirled with vibrant color as the stream twisted it's way down her arm . She began to laugh and vigorously shook her head so the water on top would soak into her hair . She sprung up to her feet a began to walk toward the butterflies and paused .

" Is it alright ? "

Wayne nodded and smiled . She approached the swarm and reached her hand into the fray . A aqua winged landed on her palm . The sensation was strange but pleasant , a soft tingling and pulsating feel as it walked around on her bare skin . She giggled and softly raised her hand to set it on it's way . It departed and returned to the dance . She stared into the spectacle for what seemed like an eternity . She had become soaking wet . Her shirt clung to her revealing the womanhood it once hid .

" It is about time for you to be heading on . " Wayne's voice snapped her out of the daze that she was in . " You have places to be and we have things to do . "

She walked back toward the couch and nodded . John was fast asleep on Wayne's lap , a smile painted on his face . Wayne took a massive hit and blew a puff of green smoke at Jules . It engulfed her and the forest faded from her view . She once again was floating in a cloud of serene smoke . Her mind drifted in and out . Flashes of her early childhood filled her mind then rushed away before she could make sense of them . " Stacey . " she whispered and the smoke began to churn . " I'll find you . I'll find all off you . "

Chapter 56

Mathew lost sight of Grace's car as she turned of Spencer road onto Spruce Lane . He floored it . The sounds of his sirens echoing off the surrounding houses . He grabbed the radio in another attempt to get her to calm down and stop running .

" Grace . Come on just stop the car . We can work through this , just you and me . Grace answer me . "

He turned on to spruce . Grace's car was parked on the street . He pulled in behind it and got out . The drivers door was open . Mathew looked into the car . Her clothes were lying in a pile on the passenger seat . Her badge sat on top , but here gun was no where to be seen . He looked around the neighborhood in hopes of spotting her .

A crashing noise from the house on the corner got his attention .

" What is she doing at Andy's house ? "

He ran across the street and down to the source of the noise . A metal trash can had been knocked over . Andy's trash was scattered across his yard , old torn up porn magazines , empty boxes of frozen dinners , an offer for a free hair cut at Snazzy Snips . No sign of Grace .

Mathew drew his gun and slowly proceeded to the house . The front door was ajar . He slowly pushed it open with his free hand and whispered . "Grace . "

A black mass jumped out the door at Mathew . In a moment of panic , he fired two shots at it in reflex and spun around to see what he hit .

A blue cat laid panting on the ground , a butterfly covered bandana around it's neck . It looked at him with disgust and showed off his claws and fangs in protest to being shot .

" Felix ! "

The sound of glass breaking came from with in the house . Mathew kicked the door open and stepped in , glancing over his shoulder as he entered .

Felix had two fresh bullet holes through his side , yet he

stood up , shook it off and ran down the road , singing a haunting song in a language foreign to Mathew's ears .

Mathew made his way to the back of the house searching room to room as he went . He opened the master bedroom door to see Sabrina lying on the bed , naked , a cell phone next to her . The patio door was shattered . A chair on the other side the obvious culprit .

Mathew ran through the opening . A cloaked figure was running through the back yard heading for Spencer Road . He took of after her and fired a shot in the air .

" Stop or I will shoot you . "

A soft rain began to fall . The waxing moon was near it's apex .

The woman continued to run , ignoring the shot and his warning . She reached the road and turned for Spencer bridge . Mathew slowly gained on her . She made it to the foot of the bridge and Mathew fired another warning shot . He was with in fifty feet of her and still closing .

" Seriously stop ! I have had it with all this running . "

She slowed her pace as she approached the middle of the bridge . Mathew aimed his gun at her .

" Stop and turn around . This mad night is going to end . Turn around before I loose my cool ! "

She stopped and took a deep breath . She looked over her shoulder at him and lowered her hood .

" Casidy ! "

" Hello dad . "

" Why ? Did that woman touch you ? "

She smiled . Her black lips formed lines that told Mathew he did not know his daughter at all .

" What woman ? "

" Pandora . "

" Never heard of her . I am doing this for my own reasons . I am following my own path . "

" Raping girls and taunting me . Is this your way of punishing me ? "

" What makes you think this is about you ? You abandoned Z and I a long time ago . You are dead to me . "

Mathew lowered his gun . His hands were trembling ,
anguish ran through his veins . He loved his girls but lost
sight of them in his own personal hell . He discovered his
wife did not love him far before the scandal . He distanced
him self from the girls little by little for the reminded him of
the source of his torment especially Casidy . She was so
much like her mother , beautiful , willful , playful and sassy
and now he knows he has lost her for good as well .

" Let's just go home . We will work this out sweety .
Please . "

He dropped his gun and reached out his hand to her but
she slapped it away .

" I hate you . Now suffer . "

She turned her head away from him and sprinted for the
edge of the bridge . He jumped to grab her but she eluded
him and reached her launch point , the same spot her mom
dove from only three days ago . She soared out of his site ,
tears falling behind her in streams chasing her down into
oblivion . Her last thought . " I am so sorry Z . "

Mathew fell to his knees and screamed .

" Oh god no ! What did I do ! "

He sat there and cried . His world had been nearly
destroyed . How was he going to explain this to Zia . Would
he loose her too ?

" Mathew . "

He stood up to see a figure walking up the bridge . It was
Grace . She was naked and had a blank look on her face .
Her gun dangled in her left hand .

" I figured it out . "

He wiped his eyes and took a breath . " What ? "

She aimed the gun at his head and pulled the trigger . He
was hit between the eyes and fell , blood pouring from his
head as he hit the road . She walked up beside him , put the
gun to her head and ended her life as well , her last
moments frozen for eternity with the man she was obsessed
with .

Diary of Casidy Rain

Monday

Dad was screaming at mom . He called her a filthy whore and other horrible names . That bitch Grace was there nodding her head . Who the hell is she ?

I tried get them to leave her alone , but mom just smiled at me and said it was fine . Fine ? What the fuck did she me fine ? How could she let him treat her that way ? All the things he has done to her over the years never seemed to faze her . Doesn't she care ?

I overheard Persephone and mom taking . What was she doing playing with herself in the woods ? She has always had some interesting quirks but wow . Dad still had no business treating her like that . So what if got horny and took a break . Why is everyone making such a big deal out of it ?

Tuesday

I saw them . Dad and Grace were kissing in his car . Did mom know what hey were up to ? Should I tell her ? No . She is hurting enough . That bastard has lost the last bit of my respect .

Mom just sits in her chair , staring out the window . I tried to talk to her but she just sent me away and went back to staring . Am I loosing her ? What about Z , is she ok ? I am starting to get scared .

Wednesday

What a strange dream . Three of my friends from school Heather , Lilith and Sabrina dancing around naked in the forest . They looked pretty happy as they blew me kisses . A cloaked figure was in the middle of them . It was a girl but I could not see her face . When I woke up , mom was standing over me . She looked very sad and my heart sunk as she sighed . She didn't say anything . She just brushed the hair from my eyes and walked out . I got up and looked for her but she was nowhere to be found .

Persephone is watching us tonight . She said mom needed sometime to think . She has always struck me as a little odd . I like her but she doesn't seem to fit . She spent the entire night playing games with Zia . They seem pretty attached to one another . I am glad Z has her as a friend . She doesn't have many . She is just to shy for her own good . But I love her no matter .

Thursday

I can't breath . Please someone just kill me . Why mom ? How could you leave Z and I alone ? How could you jump of a bridge with me watching ? Please god let me be in a dream . I don't understand . I thought she was strong . He did this . He drove her to kill her self . I hate him . He deserves to burn .

Friday

I must have been screaming from the nightmares I was having . Z shook me awake then climbed onto the bed with me . She stroked my face and told me everything was going to be ok . If it were anyone else , I would have slapped her for saying such a thing . It will never be ok . But Z is my treasure . She only wants to make me feel better . I kissed her cute forehead and told her I would be fine . I don't think she believed me . She insisted on staying with me the rest of the day .

Saturday

The funeral . It was unbearable . Seeing my dad and that bitch Grace getting all cozy at they are putting my mom in the ground . Unforgivable . And those smug Solomons , with their fake sense of concern . Hypocritical monsters , they helped drive mom to her end .
I lost it . Sorry mom , but I had to say something .

I just wanted to sleep . I was to tired to be angry anymore . Then my day had to go and get weirder . Persephone gave me a box that mom had left for me . What was mom thinking ? Did she loose her mind and go insane ? A black silk cloak with a moon on the hood . Ok I can deal with that . A bit odd but cool . A tranquilizer gun though , what the hell is that for ? Why would she leave me such a thing .

That dream . I understand now . There is something I have to do for mom . Something that was very important . I don't know why just that it was mom's wish and that is good enough for me . Poor Z though . Felix was precious to her . What a horrible week . I want to help her get through this but now I have no time . Please forgive me Z .

Lily was at the park . Persephone and Zia made this easy by letting me stay . Heather lived not ten minutes walk from here . I hung with Lily and Brad for a few then excused myself and made my way to my first target . I shot her . Wow , I really shot her . Concern ran through my mind . I certainly did not want to cause her harm . She was cool . I took her out of the light a stripped her . The effects of the tranquilizer seemed to wear off a little . She was awake as I made love to her . It was amazing . I could sense a massive release in energy with in her as we both had an a orgasm . I never would have forced someone to have sex with me before now . I was very relieved that she enjoyed it and held no ill toward me . My path was set .
I made my way back to the park and hung out awhile longer then had Lily take me home . Z was reading a large old book . I asked her about it but she fibbed to me .

History book my ass . I didn't even recognize the language .
Oh well , she just didn't want to bore me with it I guess .
Then he came home . I knew we were about to go at it and
that was fine with me . He slapped me . I dropped and
started crying , but it was just a show . He couldn't hurt me
any more than he already has . Z jumped to my side . Damn
she is quick . She pulled my head to her bosom and tore
into dad . She smelled divine . I could feel the fury flowing
through her and it turned me on . The longer I sat there the
more tempting she became . If I didn't get out of there I
would have taken her to the ground and had my way with
her . That would have probably killed dad . He left and she
let me go , just in time . I had to leave . I went out the door
and stole dad crotch rocket then headed to Ray's for some
food .

Lilith . I empathize with her . I understand the desire to
die . But it is not the answer . I know that now . I convinced
her to let me have her . She was very enjoyable and went
out with a smile on her face . Now the hard one . How do I
get to Sabrina ?

Wow . Seems like there is more going on than my little
quest . That girl Domino solved my problem . She got Andy
to chase her past me . I shot that bitch once in the neck
then another into his leg for good measure . She got his
keys and threw them to me . How did she know I needed
them ? Why was she helping me ?

I got into Sabrina's with no problems . She was sitting on
her bed naked . She smiled when she saw me and told me
she knew I was coming for her , something about a dream .
That settled it . I have no more fear of how this ends . This is
bigger than me and I will finish what I started . I made love
to her as well . I had become pretty satiated by this point .
Three girls in one night , got to be a record . The sound of a
gun going off startled me . I tried to open the patio door
but it was locked so I grabbed a chair and threw it through

the window . I ran out and made my way to the bridge .
Dad came out the window behind me . This was perfect . I
can make him suffer for all that he has done . I let him catch
up to me as I got close to my launch point . He was going
to shoot me . That would have been lame . I let him see who
I was before leaping from the bridge . I could hear him
scream as I fell into the darkness . I am coming Z . Please
catch me .

  Random images filled my mind . I was immersed in cold
water . Trees drifted passed me . Blackness then a small
point of light . I am on the ground . I feel rain on my face .
My eyes open and a blurry face is looking down at me . A
small soft hand caressed my forehead .
  " Welcome back to the land of the living my sweet sister . "

Chapter 58

Tears rolled down Vander's face as he sat staring at the marble figure in the corner of the room . The shock of his mother's murder was wearing off and reality was setting in . Daniel and Samantha entered the game room .

" Vander sweety , we are so sorry . "

Samantha put her arms around him and kissed him on top of the head . He didn't flinch . He continued to stare at the silent lady in front of him , focusing on her cold eyes .

" Let him be Sam . We need to give him some space . "

Vander stood up and faced them .

" No . I will be fine eventually . Thanks for the hug Sam . "

" I would do any thing for you and Domino . "

A black pulsating sphere materialized in front of Daniel . It quickly expanded and dissipated as Agamemnon and Persephone stepped from it .

Vander went from sad to angry . He pointed his finger at them .

" Where where the two off You ?! . You let my mom die . She trusted you and you let her die ! "

He stomped his foot and colors flashed across his eyes . The room started disintegrating into thousands of colored lines . Daniel grabbed Sam and pulled her away from Vander . Persephone began to form a black sphere in her hand but Agamemnon grabbed her arm and shook his head then looked at Vander .

" Pattern . Your mom awoke the way of patterns in you and this is how you use it . Are you going to kill us all ? Do you hate us that much ? How about Sam and Daniel ? If you continue they will die as well . "

Vander calmed down and the room settled into a twisted version of its former self .

" I am sorry . I didn't mean to do that . Just tell me why . "

" It sucks to be powerless . I would have given my life to save Miranda . You are right . She trusted us and we let her down . Out here all I can do is watch . I am no match for

Donovan as long as I am bound . I understand your anger . Please forgive us . "

" I want someone to pay for what happened . I should not have aimed my anger at you . I am just frustrated . I feel powerless too . "

" We will make them pay . "

Domino was standing in the door way . She had a serious look on her face . Vander stared into his four year old sisters eyes wondering if she understood what had happened .

" Someday we will , even if it takes my last breath . I have waited over four centuries for their fall and I will wait another four if that is what it takes . They will meet their end . " Agamemnon studied Domino carefully .

" No . Not four centuries . I will make them fall . I know the path to the end of the veil . I know how to stop the architects . "

" You know the path ? Explain . "

" I see future scenarios , different outcomes based on choices that will present themselves . I tried to find a quick and easy path to the end of this horror , but none exist . I pushed further into time and came up with the start of a solution . I couldn't get to the end . My head is throbbing . The further I tried to go the worse the pain got . "

" I have never heard of a way like that . The weight of the veil is starting to work against itself . Too many people with too much curiosity is causing it to waver . You are the answer to its end . How far did you get ? "

" Nine years from now . I know everything that needs to happen in that span of time . " She handed Agamemnon a writing tablet . " Only read the pages on the date that I wrote on them . Don't read ahead or it will all fail . It will require a lot of sacrifices . " She looked at Samantha . " I am very sorry your part in this . It will work out in the end though . I know it . "

" My part ? What do you mean ? "

" Sorry . Can't say right now . " She turned to Agamemnon . " Vander and I need to forget everything until the right time . Do so then read the first page . "

" Understood . "
He formed a black sphere and expanded it into a portal .
" We need to go to the void . I need to use pattern . "
They were all standing in blackness and silence .
Agamemnon's eyes danced with color and the two young
Stars memories faded away .

" Wake up Vander . " Domino ran her fingers through his hair .

He awoke from his dream and sat up . Specks of colors flowed over his eyes . He looked around the room with a sense of wonder . He saw the strands of energies that everything was composed of and the patterns they were arranged in to create their reality . His attention shifted as Domino sat her hand on his shoulder .

" You knew , didn't you ? "

" Ya . I remembered everything when Pandora touched me . "

" Then how could you ... "

She put her finger to his mouth . " Not now . We have to go . Let Violet and Alexis sleep . " She grabbed his hand and climbed off the bed . They made their way out of Moonscape and headed down the road .

" Where are we going ? "

" To get the rest of our family . "

" Family ? You mean like your brother that you coerced into bed ? "

" It was necessary . You remember now don't you ? Why do you think that is ? Not to mention , if I didn't get laid my head was going to literally explode . "

" Oh ya , the head aches . Kind of a kinky cure don't you think ? "

" It's a huge release of tension and pent up energies . Try having thousands of scenes flow through your mind for a few hours and see how tense you get . "

" Point made . What about Violet ? "

" She will remember her past when she wakes and gain a better understanding of her way just like you did . "

" How far have you planned ? "

" No questions . To answer even the simplest one could change the outcome . "

" So what then ? Just do as you say blindly ? "

" Now you understand . "

Vander knew not to say anything else . Domino new the way and he had to trust her even if it made him uncomfortable . He was overwhelmed by his new found power but all he wanted was to see his friends safe .

" I will do what ever you ask little sister . Just promise me that I won't loose any one else that is important to me . "

" You have my word . "

Chapter 59

The rain was coming down in sheets . The moon was
totally obscured by thick dark clouds . The wind howled as
it pick up its pace . The trees swayed violently sending a
mass of leaves into the torrent winds . The party was over .
Members of Four Dragons scrambled to get their gear into
the vans and out of harms way . Black Dragon stood on the
podium pointing and shouting orders to his cohorts . He
spotted a figure dressed in white walking into the park .
There was a soft glow surrounding it which illuminated the
ground as it moved . He yelled into the mike for Lily's
attention and pointed toward the park entrance .
Lily , Brad and Veronica began to walk toward the figure .
" It's not Donovan , way to short . " Veronica said with
some relief .
" Ya , well who ever it is had better be friend and not foe or
I am going to smack them around . "
Brad grabbed lily's arm and slowed her down . " Careful
babe . I have a bad feeling about this . "
" Seriously ? If I can't handle this , I know you can . Relax
babe . "
Brad smiled and shook his head . " Quit stroking my ego . "
The figure's details became clearer . It was a old man
barely taller than Veronica . His left eye was covered in a
white film . His face was scarred and pitted . He smiled as
he approached Lily , his teeth jagged and shattered .
" Hello wicked little creatures . I am here to claim this park
in the name of my mistress Eno . Kneel and submit and I
may be kind in dealing with you vile things . "
Lily's eyes got wide as she clenched her fist . She lunged at
the man and swung for his face . " You kneel ! "
The man jumped back and laughed . He was far faster than
Lily thought he was . He threw his hands into the air and
screamed . A flying creature descended from the sky . "
Death by scissor wing , oh so fun to watch . " It was about
the size of a person and covered with dark leathery skin .

The edges of its wings were sharp and shiny . Its mouth was like a dagger when closed . It glared at Lily with its fiery red eyes as it dove at her .

Brad yelled out her name as he jumped in front of her . The scissor wing impaled him in the stomach . Pain shot through his body as he fell to the ground , his weight pulling the scissor wing down on top of him . He wrapped his arms around the monsters head and looked at Lily , tears running down his face . " Run babe . " He forced a smile as his life faded away .

Lily screamed his name and tried to run to his side but Veronica grabbed her arm and attempted to pull her away from the scene .

" No Lily ! , We have to run . "

" Brad ! Please baby get up . Brad ! "

Kenny and Curtis came running to the girls side . Kenny aimed a shot gun at the creatures head and pulled the trigger . It screamed and fell off Brad . Lily tried to get out of Veronica's grip but Kenny yelled out .

" Get her out of here Veronica ! "

Veronica tightened her grip on Lily and pulled her toward the nursery and away from immediate danger . Lily tried to resist . She wanted to be at her dads side when he made that old man pay for what he had done . But it was futile . Veronica continued to drag her away from the scene . With each step she felt lower and lower for leaving Papa K and Curtis to fend for them selves , but she knew Lily's safety was in her hands .

The old man jumped up and down in a furious fit . " You will pay for that you miserable little man ! Now die ! "

Kenny stared into the rain as the sky filled up with gleaming red eyes making their descent from the darkness above . The sounds of hundreds of piercing screams filled the air , sending shivers down Kenny's spine .

" Oh god , there are more of them Papa K . " Curtis was both scared and excited .

" Ya . We need more ammo . " Kenny's mouth formed a tight smile .

The old man began to laugh as he jumped about waving his arms in the air . A swarm of scissor wings emerged from the sky , their eyes locked on the man who downed their brother .

Kenny and Curtis opened fire on the incoming fliers . The scent of blood filled the air as a bullet ripped through one of their wings . The flier spiraled to the ground as it screamed a song of agony sending the rest of the flock into a frenzy .

The wind intensified ripping small trees from the ground and throwing them into the air like tooth picks . The rain came down so heavy that Kenny and Curtis could barely see one another .

A car approached the two at rapid speeds , its headlights barely visible as it came to a sudden stop , sliding side ways a few feet from them . The trunk flew open as Penny stepped from the car .

" What the hell are you doing girl !? " Curtis yelled as he continued to stare at the swarm coming down at them .

" What kind of girl do you think I am ? " Penny grabbed a couple of guns and made her way to his side . " I never leave my mans side , especially when he needs me . "

Kenny shook his head and started firing toward the swarm . The sounds of high pitched screams echoed through the air . " Ya . Take that you flying bitches . "

Curtis and Penny joined in . The three of them sprayed the air with bullets . The smell of blood permeated the air as scissor wings fell to the ground one after the other .

The old man became furious . He slapped his hands together as he stared at the three mortals causing him grief . The ground at their feet began to glow and the scissor wings became silent .

Kenny stopped firing . He watched as the faint red eyes in the sky began to form a line . A feeling of dread over came him . He turned to his friends . " Run ! "

Chapter 60

Zia and Persephone stood on the bank of the river watching Casidy's body float toward them . Persephone stepped into the river , grabbed the corpse and threw it over her shoulder .

" Hey ! Be careful with her . " Zia was appalled .

" Easy now . She will be fine when you are done with her . "

Persephone stepped out of the water and headed into the forest , stopping when she realized that Zia had not moved . " Um , are you coming ? "

Zia stared at her sister . She was bruised and cut all over . Her beautiful blond hair covered in slime . It took Zia every ounce of will not to break into tears . She took a deep breath and followed Persephone . " Ya . Just didn't realize how horrified I would get seeing her like this . "

The two of them walked for a few minutes until they were in a small clearing . Heather , Sabrina and Lilith were there . They were naked and wet with smiles painted on their faces . The sight of Casidy's dead body did not seem to phase them . It was if they knew all was well .

Persephone laid Casidy on the ground and stepped away . Zia knelt next to her and straightened up Casidy's clothes the best she could . She then asked that her naked assistants form a triangle around the two of them .

When everyone was in place , Zia stood up . She closed her eyes and whispered something into the wind . Her butterflies began to glow intensely and landed on Casidy . Strands of ethereal thread encased her and became solid forming a cocoon . A bright light began to shine from with in . The silhouette of hundreds of flying butterflies covered the surface of the cocoon .

Gossamer wings appeared on the three girls as the cocoon began pulsating showering the area with a barrage of colors . The sensation was incredible . They felt truly alive and unbound .

Zia fell to her knees and put both hands on the cocoon .

The pulsating intensified . It got faster and faster until the cocoon exploded . Butterflies shot into the open air dancing in between rain drops . The girls fell to the ground and laughed , pleasure coursing through them .

Zia stroked Casidy's forehead and she opened her eyes .

" Welcome back to the land of the living , my sweet sister . I am so very happy to see you again . "

Casidy sat up slowly and looked around . Her head was spinning and nothing seemed quite real . She pinched her self and jumped at the shock of pain . " Guess I am alive . " She looked into Zia's eyes . They were sad and scared . " You brought me back . Some how I knew you would . "

Zia wrapped her arms around Casidy and began to shake . Everything finally caught up with her . She held her self together up to that point because she could not afford to make a mistake , but with Casidy in her arms she could let go .

" I am so sorry . Watching you be miserable broke my heart . Please know that I didn't have a choice . Please forgive me . "

Casidy pulled Zia onto her lap and kissed her on the lips . The sensation was overwhelming . She tasted so sweet , so tempting , Zia's lips and tongue became everything . She tightened her embrace and deepened the kiss . Erotic images flashed through her mind as bliss made its way through her .

Zia became very relaxed . This was her first real kiss and it was with her treasure . Her sadness faded and was replaced by joy . Casidy was fine and still loved her . All was well with Zia's universe .

Casidy released her lock on Zia's lips and softly stroked the side of her face . She smiled and shook her head .

" I could never be angry with you Z , I love you too much and I know how much you love me . I trust you . You did what you did because it was important . I know you would never do anything against me . "

" Thank you . You are my treasure and I am here to make you happy . I am here to complete you . "

Chapter 61

Penny drug Curtis toward the pond as blood poured from the gash in his leg . Kenny walked backwards trying to cover them but the scissor wings were coming in fast and hard . Leathery bodies on the ground were a testament to Kenny's tenacity but he had reached his limits . The opposition was too much for him to handle .

A line of scissor wings made a dive for the three of them . Kenny and Penny dropped to the ground in hopes of making them selves harder targets .

" I am sorry kids . God help us . " Kenny knew it was the end .

The air suddenly became still as Reginald came into view . He raised his hand to the air and lightning bolts shot down from the sky , frying a handful of fliers . The screeching sounds of pain echoed through the air as freshly cooked corpses fell to the ground . The rest of the column broke off and scrambled trying to get out of harms way .

Reginald quickly made his way to Kenny and the others . He looked up into the sky and the storm began to calm down . He smiled at Kenny then looked toward the old man .

" I've got this . You three just chill . "

He slowly walked toward the old man keeping his eyes locked on him , pointing his finger at him as he got closer .

" It is over old man . Surrender and I will spare your life . "

" Foolish little boy . Who do you think you are ! I am Ketin , agent of the Architect's ! No one speaks to me like that . "

Ketin pointed toward Reginald . " Kill him ! "

The remaining scissor wings turned toward their target and made a simultaneous dive at Reginald . He smiled and shook his head . He waited until they were all close then slapped his hands together . A wave of flame flew toward the incoming fliers and in a flash the sky lit up with burning corpses . They fell from the air like the after effects of fireworks .

" H ... How , how can you posses the way of elements ? " Ketin turned and began to run .

" I don't think so . I gave you your chance . " Reginald formed a fire ball in his hand and threw it at Ketin . It hit , setting him a blaze . Ketin ran in circles for a moment , screaming in agony until he collapsed and went silent .

A sense of satisfaction flowed through Reginald but was quickly dampened by the smell of burning flesh . Hill park was safe for the moment . He did what Domino asked of him and he was ready to see his family again . He helped Kenny and Penny to their feet and took a deep breath .

" Sorry I didn't get here sooner . " He glanced at Brad's body . " Too much pain for one night . I hope it gets easier but I'm not holding my breath . "

" Ya . I feel you . " Curtis forced a smile through the pain . " Guess I am lucky I'm still alive . You saved our asses . You must be another one of Domino's friends . "

" You know Domino ? What other friends ? "

Curtis started laughing . Sharp pains shot through his leg with each chuckle but they only made him laugh harder . Every thing that had happened that evening had caught up to him . He realized his world was gone and replaced with something new , something dangerous and exciting . He learned some things about him self as well , like how strong he could be when needed and how he was part of something much larger than him self .

" Ya . I know her . She is one hell of a girl and those other friends of yours are pretty amazing as well . "

" Please , do you know where I can find them ? "

Curtis took a deep breath and calmed him self down . He was feeling a little woozy from loss of blood . He had been riding on adrenaline but that was fading . " The Moonscape . I left them there before the party . "

" Hush love . You need to rest . " Penny finished wrapping his wound with cuttings from her shirt .

" Ya . Rest my friend . Thank you for the info . It's time I go find my family . " Reginald turned and made his way out of the park waving behind him as he departed .

Chapter 62

Zia and Casidy stood , holding hands . The rain softly fell upon them , a much more soothing feeling than the down pour of earlier . Casidy's turmoil was over . Her mind was clear and her path now set in stone . She kissed Zia on the fore head .

" Let's do this . "

Zia nodded and motioned to the girls . They got up off the ground and brushed themselves off . Then in unison , flew up a bit and over to their positions . As they slowly flapped their wings , a scent of sweet flowers spread through the air .

Casidy inhaled , smiled and tightened her grip on Zia's hand . Her heart was racing from sensory over load . The smell ,the rain , the touch of her sisters hand were enough make her head swim . She was starting to understand what true joy was and she wanted more .

Zia began whispering to the wind . The butterflies formed a circle around the triangle . She kissed Casidy's hand then released it . Images of Samantha , Wayne and John flashed in and out in the center . Zia's whispers got louder . The butterflies flew clock wise in the circle and the images became stronger and stronger until the images became real and solid .

Wayne and John stood at each side of Samantha . A smile crossed their faces as their gaze fell on Zia and Casidy .

" A pleasure little ones . Exciting night , yes ? " Wayne looked around to survey the scene . " Mistress Persephone , it has been a long time my friend . "

" Too long . " Persephone was leaning against a tree . " We can reminisce later . It is time to raise Sam . Now come over here and get out of the circle . Let the new keepers finish their task . " She waved them to her .

" So it is true . After so long , the universe has given us not one but two keepers . It is truly a blessed day for all of fairy kind . " John was pleased . The suffering of his people was about to come to an end . The future of fairy kind was now in the hands of two young girls .

Zia and Casidy placed their hands on Samantha . The butterflies broke the circle and landed on Sam . Casidy and Zia stood and raised their hands to the air . Ethereal threads wrapped around Sam and formed a cocoon . The girls wings began to spread glittering fairy dust into the air . As some of it settled on the cocoon it began to pulsate . Colors filled the air and the scent of bliss aroused all who where present .

The cocoon exploded and Samantha opened her eyes . Casidy and Zia helped her to her feet . They wrapped their arms around her . Casidy lost her composure and began to cry .

" I missed you so much . I was so confused . I didn't know how I was going to survive loosing you . "

Sam ran her fingers through Casidy's hair . A tear ran down her face . To put her girls through all of this was maddening and unbearable . She couldn't stand to see them in pain .

" I am so sorry baby . I swear , if there was another path we would have taken it , but you needed the grief to open up your way . I love both of you dearly . Please forgive me . "

" Of course I do . I am just happy the three of us are back together . "

Persephone sighed and shook her head . " Sorry kitten , but your mom's path is not yours . The two of you are special . You have a unique path and a vital one at that . You are the keepers , keepers of fairy kind . "

Casidy looked into Sam's eyes unsure of how she felt . " Is that true ? We get you back and you are leaving us again ? "

" I am afraid so at least for a little while . We will see each other , I promise , but Persephone is right . Our paths are not the same . The two of you will be fine . You have each other . Please be strong . This is far bigger than just us . The world needs us . "

Casidy released her embrace , grabbed Zia's hand and pulled her away from Sam . " I understand mom . I am just glad you are with the living . We will do our part . " She smiled and pulled Zia close . " Everything is fine . I have my treasure and I know my mom is alright . We will do our part . Just point is in the right direction "

Sam turned to Persephone . " It is time . Bring them to me . Let's see what I am capable of . "

" Yes . I am eager to see the fruits of our labor . "

Chapter 63

Donovan looked around the empty field while studying the coin . It sensed the presence of an awakened was near by but the only life in sight was a few rodents scurrying about . He was soaking wet and annoyed . His night had been full of misfortunes and he was growing tired of his failures .

He knew his days were numbered if he continued to fail his mistress . Eno was not the most patient person . If he didn't step up and show his worth , she would surely make an example out of him .

The hairs on his body came to attention as the ground exploded near his feet . He jumped back and pulled out his dagger . His eyes quickly scanned the scene . As he turned his head , Jules unleashed another cutting wave toward him . He barely dodged as the ground was ripped apart .

" So we meet again little thing . It seems you have more control over your way this time . "

Jules waved her hand toward him emitting another threshold wave at him . " I am going to kill you . I am going to make you pay for the pain you have caused . "

He leaped toward her trying to get close enough to sap her power but she was wise to him and teleported behind him . He turned just in time to avoid another wave .

" So , you know to keep your distance . You are not a stupid as I thought or are you . " He leaped toward her while throwing his dagger at the ground behind him . Jules teleported again landing almost on top of the dagger .

Her energy suddenly waned as she collapsed to the ground . She struggled to breath and started to crawl away from the dagger . Darkness began to fill her eyes .

" How utterly pitiful . All that power and no brains . What kind of moron awakens babies . " He casually walked toward her . " Time to die you stupid little hack . "

A soft laugh came from Jules mouth . She rolled over onto her back and shook her head . " You loose . "

Donovan stopped in his tracks . He had her down and drained of energy . How can she say something like that and be calm about it .

" What are you talking about ? "

The temperature suddenly dropped and Donovan began to shiver . His heart sunk into his chest and as a feeling of dread overcame him .

" She is talking about me . Care to finish what you started bitch ? "

Donovan turned around to see Stacey staring him down . Before he could flinch she surrounded him in ethereal form . Terror shot through his mind as images of his victims began to unravel his sanity .

Jacob got to Jules . The dagger didn't seem to have any effect on him as he picked it up and tossed it away from Jules . Her energy quickly returned as she got to her feet .

" Thanks sweety . Stacey ! Let me finish this . "

Stacey smiled and backed away from Donovan . Jules eyes began glowing bright white . She slashed her hand through the air and thousands of mirrored planes appeared . She pointed at Donovan and the thresholds intersected him from every angle . He was trapped in a thousand pockets of space .

Jules lowered her hand and threshold pieces began to disappear taking chunks of Donovan with them . His face was frozen in agony . His eyes accusing as they vanished from view . Donovan was no more . His corpse sent off in pieces to unknown places .

The sound of clapping filled the air . Jules turned to see Domino and Vander walking toward them .

" I am impressed . My family will never fall . We are all spectacular . "

Jules ran to Domino and embraced her . Jacob and Stacey followed . The Stars had come back together . The night was over and all went as Domino predicted .

" Let's go home . " Domino turned and began walking . Her entourage on her heals . " Now we are complete . Now the fun begins . "

Chapter 64

Persephone placed her hands together . She then slowly pulled them apart , forming a black swirling sphere . It drifted a few feet from her then expanded forming a portal to the void .

" I never thought I would see this day . Every since Domino laid out her plan , I wondered if she was sane . Since then I came to realize she is brilliant . That girl was responsible for moving so many pieces on a complex board . Now we finally have a chance to fix what was broken so long ago . "

" Then why do you look so tense all the sudden Persephone ? " Zia smiled as she gripped Casidy's hand tighter .

" I have almost forgotten what I am capable of with out bindings . I am a little nervous , excited but nervous . "

The portal pulsated as figures began to emerge . Agamemnon was the first to appear followed by Daniel , Ivan , Tempest and finally Pandora . Agamemnon embraced Persephone and sighed .

" I have missed you my love . A decade is a long time to be hollow , even considering the centuries we spent together . You are as radiant as ever . "

" I know . Thanks to all our young friends , we can finally see the end of our woes . "

Agamemnon released his embrace and turned to Samantha .

" I am glad to see you are well Sam . I am also very pleased to finally meet your daughters . They are both brave and lovely girls . " He smiled at the two of them . " I wish we could all chat for awhile but I am afraid time is on a leash . Samantha , it is time to test your way . "

Agamemnon took off his shirt . His chest and arms were covered in ropes of glyphs . Sam approached him then laid her hands on his chest . The glyphs began to glow and vibrate . As the vibrations intensified , the glyphs began to crack until they came unraveled completely . Agamemnon screamed as the energies that were locked away returned to him . His eyes filled with a chaos of colors swimming in the deepest black . His presence began to flow freely . It's intensity sent a chill down the spines of all around him . Even Persephone was momentarily uneasy .

" Amazing ! I had forgotten who I am . You are a true marvel Sam . I am very eager to see what your girls are capable of . "

His presence evened out to the relief of his onlookers . He took a deep breath . His mind was racing with the long forgotten sensation he was now feeling . He motioned for Sam to unravel Tempest bindings .

Tempest disrobed completely . Her body was covered in various glyphs from her ankles to her neck . Sam pulled her close and wrapped her arms around Tempest . She then delivered a deep kiss to Tempest lips . The glyphs began to glow as before but got very hot , burning Tempest skin . They had a tight hold on her and intended to make her pay for trying to remove them .

Tempest wanted to scream . The pain was becoming unbearable as she tried to get free of Sam's grip . Sam only held her tighter . The glyphs began to crack as Tempest started loosing consciousness until finally they all broke away and Tempest blacked out .

Sam handed Tempest to Agamemnon .

" Here . Look after her while I deal with Persephone . "

Persephone had already removed her shirt . The glyphs were only around her navel and upper arms . She looked at Wayne and smiled .

" Your vixen worked well my friend . It blocked a lot of the binding . With out it we would never had been ale to pull all this off . "

" It was the least I could do my lady . "

Sam placed her hand on Persephone's belly . The glyphs gave virtually no resistance . They loosened quickly and with in seconds they vanished with out a fuss .

Persephone could feel her energy return . Four centuries had lulled her into becoming comfortable with her limited self but now she was truly alive . Her mind drifted to thoughts of Eno . How they were once inseparable but now brutal enemies . She looked at Casidy and Zia . She remembered how that closeness felt and how bad it hurt when she was betrayed by the person she loved most .

" I am staying with the girls . Sam's place is with Daniel . I won't leave them . Not now . They need some one to teach them their new roles . "

Wayne sighed and shook his head . " No my friend . That job falls to John and I . Go be with your love . We will make sure the girls learn their ways . "

" Um . I am sure you will but the thought of leaving them bothers me . They have lost so much already . "

Zia smiled at Persephone . " It is fine my sweet friend . Don't let us keep you from living . Go be with your family . Just make sure to pop in and say hi when you can . "

" Thank you . I love both of you dearly . I promise that I will see you soon then . " Persephone walked to the girls and gave them both a hug . " I have faith in you . "

Chapter 65

The parishioners made their way into St . Malachi's unaware of the web they were about to be tangled in . Margret stood behind the podium and watched her new flock come into view . She was the religious adviser to the masses now . The thought of how much power she wielded turned in her mind . A wicked smile crossed her face .

Eno and Gyslia sat behind her . Their mere presence was enough to keep the parishioners in check . As the last of them entered and settled down Gyslia turned to Eno and sighed .

" Mistress , I apologize for the failure at Hill park . "

" It is not your fault . I learned what I wanted . Now I know what kind of resistance to expect . It was worth the sacrifice . " Eno nodded toward the crowd before them . " Pitiful little things . Are they not ? "

" Yes mistress . "

" To blindly follow something in the name of faith is laughable . Yet , it is exactly that trait in people that allows the Veil to stand . "

" It is sad . "

" For them . Let's see what that hag can do with them . "

Margret tapped on the mike . The crowd got very quiet .

" I am sad today . Our beloved Victor has passed from this life . He died by the actions of a fiend , a wicked wicked woman . "

The crowd began to stir , some calling out words of shock and dismay , but Margret held her hand up then lowered it . They returned to stillness .

" There is great evil around us , true demons with real power . They were lured here by the wickedness that we have ignored too long , the whores who walk our streets , the homosexuals and other deviants that pervert nature , the drug users who destroy their souls with poisons , the twisted who deny God and seek demonic powers for themselves . These wicked people have brought hell to our door step . They reek of sin and are not worthy of God's grace . We can not stand for this any more . " She pounded her fist on the podium . " We must rise and do God's will . Do you understand what is at stake here ? Are you one of God's children ? The wickedness will spread if left unchecked . They are already trying to pervert your children . They spread there lies with words like freedom and choice . They seek to destroy all of God's glorious work with their vile ways . Are you God fearing ? Then rise up ! Find the wicked were they sleeps ! Drag them into the streets and show them what we do to God's enemies ! "

   The crowd erupted into raised fist and shouts of agreement . She nodded back at them and pounded her fist again . They went silent . She delighted in the control she had over them . This was her calling . She was the mouth of the divine .

   " I give you a mission , a mission ordained by God . Seek them out . Rid us of the Devil's children . No more can we restrain ourselves . We must defend the righteous from the wicked before they corrupt more souls . I see the fire of the divine in all off you . Rise up ! " She waved her hands up . " Rise up ! "

The crowd got to it's feet . " Now go . It is God's day . Now do God's work ! "

   They started filtering from their seats and out the door . Hate and fury flowed from them in waves . They were psyched up , ready to hunt and destroy all who led lives they did not agree with .

   Eno turned to Gyslia and smiled . " See , they are so easy to manipulate , a few well spoken words and they would do any thing . "

   " Yes mistress . It is amusing though . "

   " Yes love , it is . "

Chapter 66

Lily stared into the mirror in the girls bathroom . She stripped off her party clothes and threw them to the floor then removed the bindings holding her pigtails in place . Her hair fell down past her shoulders . Tears flowed liberally from her eyes as she pondered on the meaning of Lily . What was she with out her golden boy ? She never had the chance to tell him how much he meant to her . She took it for granted that he would always be at her side . How could she be so naive ?

A knock on the door snapped her out of her dazed state .

" Lily . Are you alright ? Say something please . "

She took a deep breath and looked toward the door .

" I will be fine Veronica . Give me a few minutes to pull it together . "

" Sure . We are all here for you . Take your time . "

Lily looked back at the mirror . She knew she could not stand there for ever . She open Brad's suitcase and pulled out some of his clothes . A black pair of cargo pants , Black t-shirt , combat boots and a black leather beret .

" You always wanted to see me in black didn't you love ? This is for you babe . "

She made her way out of the rest room and crossed the parking lot . She looked around at the mayhem and destruction that was before her . Brad's body laid on the ground covered with a Four Dragon's banner . Several guest were on the ground having their wounds treated by Penny , Melony and Jade . The pond was contaminated with debris and scissor wing corpses . Her world was trashed .

Veronica made her way to Lily and embraced her .

" What can I do to make you feel better ? "

" I don't want to feel better . I need to hurt for awhile . " She gently pushed Veronica away . " Will you grab a sapling from the nursery for me , the dark glory blossom please . I need to do something . "

" Um , of course . " Veronica headed to the nursery at her

friends request .

Lily made her way to Brad and knelt down . She pulled the cover from his head and kissed him . " I am so sorry babe . I will not let them get away with this . I will make you proud of me . " She got up and headed to the platform . She climbed up the ladder and looked around at her peers . It was her doing that brought them all into this mess . Now she had to ask even more of them . She grabbed the microphone and began to speak .

" I am sorry . "

Her voice echoed across the park . Everyone paused what they were doing and looked in her direction in anticipation of her next words .

" I am sorry that I put all of you in harms way . I got caught up with the promise of some excitement with out thinking about the consequences . I have always been about the joy ride , a moment of being thrilled or pleasured . I was naive . I thought the party could go on for ever with out ever having to pay a price . Everything has a price and sometimes it is far to high . I lost the person I cherished most because of my arrogance . It will take me a long time to forgive my self for that . I have a lot of work to do before I am worthy of forgiveness . No more party . Not until those righteous bastards have paid for their transgressions . "

The crowd began to clap and cheer . Lily was not the only one who wanted to see their new found nemesis pay for what they started .

" He said we were wicked little things , that we did not deserve life . Out of the mouth of a murderer . They say we are wicked . So be it . Let us show them what wicked is . If they think we will sit idly and let them subjugate us , then they are mad ! We have a right to choose our paths . We have a right to defend our lives . We have a right to be whom ever we choose to be and no man or woman , no god or demon , no powers that hide behind words will ever ever change that . We are born free ! We will die free ! We will fight them to the end and bring hell down upon any and all who try to harm us or subvert us . I love each and every one of you and will give my life for any of you . I am but one but together we are legion . Will you help me ? Will you stand with me ? " She dropped the mike , climbed down and made her way to Brad . She fell to her knees and looked up at her onlookers . " I beg you . Don't let him die in vain . "

Veronica sat the sapling next to Lily and nodded . " I am with you . Just tell me what to do . " She grabbed Lily by the arm and pulled her to her feet then broke the ground for Brad's grave with the shovel .The rest of her friends followed suit , each taking his or her turn confirming their dedication to dealing out some pain on their would be aggressors then removing a load of dirt from the ground . Kenny was the last . He lowered Brad into the hole then gave his daughter a hug .

" I am proud of you . "

They covered Brad in dirt and planted the dark glory blossom over him . Lily knelt and kissed the ground where he lay . Dark purple blossoms erupted from the sapling , a sign of hope for the future .

Made in the USA
Charleston, SC
27 November 2012